In the middle of the Italian Peninsula between the Po and Tiber Rivers, lies Etruria, which 2,500 years ago, was host to a most advanced civilization; that of the Etruscans. Its origins are mysterious, its language undeciphered, and its history is scarcely known to us. Yet, perhaps no other civilization has so provoked the imagination and interest of scholars.

Through her fine writing and scholarship, Giuliana Boldrini has recreated a feeling of what life was like during this obscure period, drawing her inspiration from a recently discovered Etruscan mural. Here she found the lone figure of a young sailor on a three-masted ship, whom she brings to life as Vel, the son of a wealthy Etruscan merchant.

Tarquinia, point of departure for Vel's long sea journey, is teeming with life around its port. His first stop is Populonia, city of iron, with its smelting shops and merchants' villas stretching across the gentle hills. Here there are games, soothsayers, and banquets; but ahead lie the perils of crossing a sea whose hostile waters and voyagers threaten safe passage to other lands.

This vibrant story of a once flourishing society—and its remarkable illustrations derived from Etruscan findings—will awaken young readers to an intriguing era.

THE ETRUSCAN LEOPARDS

THE
ETRUSCAN
LEOPARDS

by GIULIANA BOLDRINI

Translated by Isabel Quigly

Illustrations of Etruscan Art by J. C. Kocsis

PANTHEON BOOKS

CONTENTS

Map of Etruria — 5th Century B.C.

THE ETRUSCAN LEOPARDS

I.

VEL AULES PULENA

Vel sat crouched on the top of a crag and narrowed his eyes at the sunset. He had been there over an hour. Beyond the dead-calm sea the sky was red and cloudless, and to Vel it seemed perfect. He had often turned, as he sat there, to look at the white town spread out behind him with its sloping roofs, and streets, and squares, and its temple with colored plaster columns. He could see his own house quite plainly too, with the dark hole of its water tank on the roof and the narrow columns of the balcony on the first floor. But what he was really watching, what his heart was really set on, was not Tarquinia glowing in the sunset, nor his home that must now be buzzing with preparations; it was the sea and the sky.

"If only I could prophesy through the omens, like

*Head of a bronze statue of a
young boy; early 5th Century B.C.*

Arnth the soothsayer, who can read the will of the gods
in a sheep's liver!" Vel sighed. "Well, anyway, Apulu's
propitious, that's clear enough. There wasn't a cloud,
not a shadow of a cloud, when he went down, and there's
nothing wrong with the gulls' cries, either. I'm lucky,
our trip's beginning under the very best omens and as
sure as I'm Vel Pulena, son of Aules, I'm going to have
a marvelous voyage!"

And bursting with enthusiasm he leaped up, dark
curly head raised proudly, chest puffed out under the
light sleeveless tunic with its red border, a present his
father had brought back from his last voyage along the
coast of Africa.

Vel drew breath at last, and just then thought he
heard someone calling from the road that wound
around the crest of the hill from Tarquinia. Yes, some-

one was shouting; and around the bend nearest him Vel saw a skinny figure in a dark loincloth that reached just below his knees, climbing up the road and waving like a big, clumsy, broken-winged bird. "I knew it," grumbled Vel. "It's Ibico." And, sounding annoyed, he shouted "Coming!"

It was six years now since Aules had bought Ibico from a merchant in the east and installed him as Vel's tutor and watchdog; for Ibico was no ordinary slave, but a clever and cultivated Greek from one of the islands.

Ibico stopped a few steps from Vel and murmured, "The mistress sent me to look for you, sir." He had spoken in Greek and Vel answered in resigned, weary Greek as well. Greek was a great bore, with sounds so hard for an Etruscan to pronounce, but his father had told him it was the only language everyone along the coasts of the Great Sea really understood, and a good Etruscan merchant could not get along without it.

They walked home together, Vel in front and the slave a few steps behind him, as the path was too narrow for them to walk side by side; but when they reached the main road, which was deeply rutted by cartwheels, Ibico walked level with Vel.

"Is everything ready at home?" Vel asked, too excited not to talk. "Has Uncle Larnth arrived?"

"Practically ready, sir; and Larnth Pulena's carriage arrived an hour ago. The house is buzzing like a hive. The only thing needed is the garlands for the banquet hall, and the mistress is a little anxious."

Vel looked questioningly at Ibico.

"Is she *very* anxious?"

"The mistress isn't resigned to your leaving, and swears by all the gods that this journey will be unfortunate. She says she's had evil omens and that it won't be three months but three years before you and your father see your home again. And old Ninia is marching up and down like an owl hopping from branch to branch, making everyone more uneasy than ever."

Vel laughed. He knew how the cultivated Ibico disliked his old nurse, a countrywoman his mother had brought from nearby Musarna when she came to the Pulenas' house as a bride.

"But the omens are fine. The sky is red and cloudless, and I saw a seagull flying as straight as the lance of Maris. I'll tell mother."

The Greek shook his head, smiling with amusement. These superstitious Tyrrhenians! Always worrying about magic and omens as only the old countrywomen did in Ionia! But he said nothing.

They had reached the city wall that encircled Tarquinia, at the point where a rocky spur sloped down too gently and accessibly. A few peasants were still leaving through the gate, with its great architrave of square-cut stones joined so cleverly that no mortar was needed to hold them—they were held by pressure and counterpressure. The peasants were squat, sunburned and rough-haired, but gay and noisy, and were urging on asses loaded with empty baskets, because today there had been a market in the town square. The guards answered their greetings with shouts and teasing, but when Vel passed under the arch, a tall, muscular man came out of the guardroom that was cut into the thickness of the enormous walls and greeted him.

"Greetings, Vel Pulena. Are you off tomorrow?"

"Indeed we are, Aras. My father and I are sailing with the spring winds, which Poseidon is already sending propitiously from the West. It's a good wind to sail on, as everyone knows."

The commander of the gate guards laughed and bowed ironically. "And everyone knows Vel Pulena is now an experienced navigator," he said. "Old Ocno will have to hand over the rudder when you're in danger, or he'll never get the *Blue Boar* back to port."

Biting his lips, Vel gestured imperiously to Ibico and marched ahead onto the road that led straight home. Aras gave him a friendly wave, and went back into the guardroom laughing.

At a narrow road, just wide enough to take a large traveling cart, they turned and came out into a small square with a fountain in the middle—a bowl held up by a dolphin with a sickle-shaped tail.

The house had two floors and a sloping roof with cone-shaped stone decorations. Its front was rather narrow, but the wings spread sideways on either side of a long inner courtyard. The porter, who must have seen them through a spyhole, opened a single panel of the front door—the only opening on the front of the house which had no windows—and bowed. Vel ran across the hall, frightening a flock of doves that flew up in alarm, and went into a small room looking on to the pillared arcade that ran around the inner courtyard.

His mother, Ramatha, was half-lying on a couch with bronze lion's feet and a double mattress, while a slave laced her high boots of dyed leather up to the knee. Another slave was arranging her hair, which was carefully dyed blonde by a secret formula, and old Ninia, grumbling and prowling about the room, supervised the whole business. When she saw Vel, his mother put down her silver mirror and smiled at him.

Vel stopped short in the doorway checking his impulse to leap onto the couch and hug her hard.

"Aren't you lovely!" he said softly, walking around her. "You're wearing the gold necklace and earrings I like." But what he said failed to have the effect he hoped for; his mother's mouth twisted and the mirror fell to the floor.

"Oh, Vel, my darling! I wonder how long it will be before you see me dressed like this again!"

The room was suddenly in an uproar; the kneeling slave leaped up and old Ninia rushed over.

"Come, come, my lady, my love, now don't you worry yourself or you'll spoil the whole effect of the rouge. Besides, the master hates you to get upset like this."

"Ninia's quite right, my dear," someone exclaimed vigorously from the doorway. "What are you crying about now? Is this the first time a Pulena has gone to sea?"

Vel flung himself onto his father, delighted to have his support.

Aules Pulena was a tall man with the strong features of the Etruscans—long, dark, lively black eyes, and black hair to his shoulders held by the myrtle crown worn at banquets. Over his fine linen tunic he wore the *tèbennos,* the carefully folded, embroidered and painted Etruscan cloak.

Ramatha had risen and went over to her husband, taking his hand pleadingly.

"Your will is law, Aules," she said timidly, "but our son is such a child still, so very young . . ."

Vel reddened with anger and looked up into his father's face.

"Don't worry, Ramatha. Vel has reached his twelfth year today, and it's time he went through the school of experience. The sea will teach him a great deal in a short time. Now to the banquet. Are you going to keep Larnth waiting?"

Ramatha hung her head and hurried to the large banquet hall, with Ninia following breathlessly, clapping her hands, and calling the slaves in her shrill, aged voice.

II.

THE BANQUET

Aules Pulena's house was richly furnished, as a successful merchant's should be. His three cargo ships had always returned unharmed from East and West to the port of Tarquinia, loaded with merchandise. The banquet hall on the first floor looked out onto the balcony with its painted wooden pillars now encircled by wreaths of ivy and garlands of flowers. The balcony overlooked the city; down there were the paved alleyways, the thick, curving double wall with earth piled high in the middle, the steep slope to the plain through which ran the silver river; and in the distance a few huts at the port were visible and small black ships against a sky that was now pale emerald. The slaves had put white linen cloths on the tables, which stood by three low couches and the beautiful Greek vases imported from

Attica—red vases with glowing black figures of heroes and gods adorned the walls. In bronze holders set in the walls there were smoky torches, and the smell of perfumes, burned in incense holders in the form of horses and geese, competed with that of the smoke. From the ceiling hung a bronze masterpiece—a magnificent engraved lamp with thirty jets of flame spouting from burners held up by figures of men and animals.

A stout, elderly man, who looked very distinguished in his rich cloak and glittering gold earrings, was standing at one of the walls studying a well-tanned ox skin on which was a map of the shipping routes along the Tyrrhenian shores, drawn in bright red and blue—from Campania, up through high Latium, to the mouth of the river Arno, ports, inlets, and rivers were all painted with remarkable accuracy. Towards the North a curve was faintly sketched in, and at the bottom of the map was a dark red square and in Greek letters the name Massalia.

As soon as the others came into the room, Larnth Pulena stopped looking at the map and went over to them.

"Greetings, Ramatha, my wife and daughters greet you."

"Greetings, Larnth Pulena, and greetings to all your family. How are things in Tuscany?"

"Your sister-in-law is well. Our house is serene, but the goddess Uni has not heard our prayers, and no son has brought joy to our home. You and Aules are fortunate. Here's my brother with a man to take along on his journeys. Another Pulena to pursue our fortune at sea."

Vel blushed to the roots of his hair and peered suspiciously at his uncle to see if he was teasing. Larnth Pulena was good to him and Vel knew that in spite of a few slaps, he was sure of his affection. But he was a tease as well, and you could never be sure when he was serious.

Larnth took his brother by the arm and they sank down onto the double cushion of the low couch. A slave knelt to undo their sandals and put them up on the small plank that ran along under the table. Ramatha remembered her duty as mistress of the house and tried to smile and hide her sadness. Slaves came in with heavy dishes loaded with food that was either roasted or cooked in complicated sauces. The cooks were eastern slaves, and the air was full of the smell of cinnamon and spices. Vel sat down in his place, half-lying like the others, and his heart leaped with joy. For the first time he had a silver cup and a two-pronged fork with a long bone handle, like the rest. Now that he was eating at the table with his elders, using proper cutlery and drinking wine, there was no doubt about it, he was considered a man.

Throughout the banquet, while the men talked business, Vel thought of nothing but this. Larnth Pulena had been loading cargo on one of the ships since morning. A line of carts had come from Tuscany, loaded with linen beautifully woven in the Pulenas' modern factory

Sculpture;
5th-4th Century B.C.

by Egyptian clothworkers and skilled slaves. There were also soft leather sandals for men and women, and a few small jars filled with spices from faraway Persia. Vel started when he heard his mother's voice. Ramatha had risen to retire. She wanted to leave the men to talk in peace, but before she left the room she caressed Vel's head for a moment and told him not to be late for bed. Then she hurried out, and Vel saw her wiping her eyes.

Now his father and uncle were standing at the ox-skin again studying a blue curve drawn beyond the Arno, which seemed to suggest some sort of borderline.

"We've talked enough, Larnth," said Aules Pulena. "Terms as favorable as these are not offered every day. Usually we have to sell in the market wherever we land, and there's competition, especially from Carthage. This time we have a firm order from Massalia and we've got Cele Aulenna's seal to guarantee it. With two perfect ships and the best helmsman in Tarquinia, it would be folly not to attempt it."

"Well Aules, you've always known what you were doing. May Poseidon favor you. I can't come with you and I hate to leave you to face the risks alone. But I don't have a young man to leave behind and the shop is no place for a woman."

At the thought of his kind, fat aunt marching up and down through sweating, swearing weavers and slaves, Vel burst out laughing. His uncle laughed too.

"Why, Vel hasn't drunk to the success of his first voyage yet, Aules!" he cried. "D'you want him to grow up sulky or fastidious or girlish? Here, let's have some of your wine to toast his twelve years, the gods, and fair winds!"

A slave served the wine with a terra-cotta ladle from a large curved metal urn decorated all over with a hunting scene. The three Pulenas raised their cups, poured a few drops of wine onto the floor in honor of Poseidon, god of the sea, and then drank slowly. Uncle Larnth went over to the balcony and looked out to sea. The horizon was now invisible, and the only light was a feeble glimmer from a small spring crescent moon. There was no sign of the boats anchored in the port either, except for the gleaming points from the ships' lanterns. The ships had been loaded with valuable cargoes that day, and Aules Pulena's most trusted freedman was on board guarding the goods with his life.

For a long time they stood staring down at the tiny flickering light until Vel's eyelids grew heavy, and he lay down on a goatskin by the big half empty wine pot and started fiddling mechanically with its tufts of hair. He heard his father and uncle talking softly, and their tone seemed serious, almost worried. But he was very sleepy. And the last words he heard before rolling over to sleep were his uncle's.

"You won't be at sea more than a moon, Aules, but I would have sacrificed a lamb to Maris as well . . ."

"Maris? What can the god of war have to do with our journey?" Vel wondered. But before he could find an answer he was fast asleep.

III.

ON BOARD THE "BLUE BOAR"

Why was the ship rolling like this, since there were no winds and the sea was calm? It was impossible to stand upright, and one had to hold on to the rigging . . . Vel awoke with a shriek, found himself clutching his mother's dress, and she was shaking him and murmuring, "It's time to get up, Vel. Wake up!"

He sat up, suddenly.

"Where's father?"

"He's already in the courtyard, and Uncle Larnth will be down in a minute."

Vel got up and searched for his tunic and shoes, which were hard to find in the dim light of the oil lamp. Old Ninia still managed to rub his face and neck with a damp cloth while his mother, for the thousandth time, looked through his seaman's box which had his name branded on the lid. Vel saw her pull a small leather purse from the folds of her dress.

"Here are three Greek silver coins, Vel," she said. "Three coins of the city of Taranto. You've seen them sometimes." She sighed, "Don't touch them till you need them, and if you find yourself in trouble . . ."

Vel broke in with a hug. He was touched, and at the same time excited, by such a large sum. The coins were didrachmas. On one side was a dolphin with a boy on its back and on the other a horse and the word "Taras". But a slave had already heaved the box onto his stout shoulders and Vel followed him into the courtyard with his mother. It was dawn. A big cat came and rubbed against Vel's legs and he picked it up. Aules and Larnth Pulena came across to his mother, but Vel noticed another figure standing respectfully apart—his tutor Ibico. And Ibico was dressed for traveling!

"You don't mean we're taking him with us, Father!" he exclaimed in astonishment.

Aules Pulena was annoyed, and he turned to his wife without answering. Uncle Larnth laughed.

"Come, Vel! You'll have a chance to practice your Greek before you get to Massalia!" he said. "And after all, you can always throw him to the fishes."

But Ibico's presence greatly dampened Vel's enthusiasm. Farewells went on for a few more minutes, then Ramatha went back to her rooms, leaning on Ninia's shoulder, and the three Pulenas climbed into the light city carriage which had two large wheels and a single horse. Vel was clutching his cat. Earlier he had gotten permission to take her aboard, for she had proven herself a wonderful hunter, even against the huge ship rats. When Vel's father had first brought her back from Carthage, everyone in Tarquinia had been rather scared, never having seen a cat before, and Vel enjoyed boasting of the furry, agile creature he owned.

The road to the port had been paved some time before and the carriage ran fast along it, its bronze wheels clattering and throwing up sparks from the smooth stone. Then it reached the plain and followed the course of the river until it was lost among the huts huddled around the harbor. In all, it was just over a half an hour's journey for a good carriage.

The Pulenas' two cargo ships—a third was being repaired—were anchored at the port of Tarquinia, where the river met the sea. In the uncertain light of dawn the sailors were moving swiftly, shifting the final provisions, (part at least just in from Tuscany), some on deck, some on land. When Aules jumped down from the carriage, one of them came over to him; a stocky, elderly Etruscan with a great barrel chest and muscular legs, a scarred, sunburned face, and sharp eyes peering through a great mop of curly gray hair, that included beard and eyebrows, had earned him the nickname Wolf among the sailors. This was Ocno, the helmsman of the Pulenas' ships, born a sailor (according to himself) and the best on Tyrrhenian shores (according to the merchants of Cere and Tarquinia). It was years since he began working for the Pulenas, but he was a free man, not a slave, and was bound to them only by the bonds of mutual respect.

"Greetings, Aules Pulena," he called in a rich voice that had become strained from shouting orders at the crew. "This is just the time to weigh anchor—the wind couldn't be better."

He winked at Vel, and then spat so neatly at Ibico's feet that the Greek leaped back, losing his normal composure for a moment.

"So we're loading up with Greek monkeys," he said.

Ibico pointedly refused to be drawn, merely touched his unpierced ears, and, as if by chance, stared disdainfully at the large gold rings Ocno wore in his. Only thirty years earlier, these earrings were generally worn by the pirates who still infested the Great Sea, and no one could really have sworn there were no piratical feats somewhere in Ocno's past.

Aules, who had understood just what was happening, broke in impatiently,

"I'm entrusting my son to you, Ocno; you'll take him with you on the *bireme,* and I'll take the *Captain.* On board the *Blue Boar* you are father and master, and Vel will obey you as he would obey me."

Ocno replied with a gesture of agreement, and cramming a Phrygian cap with ear flaps down on his salt roughened locks, he tightened the leather belt around his worn knee-length tunic.

"Get on board, Vel," he ordered. "And carry your own box. A sailor mustn't depend on anyone else for his gear."

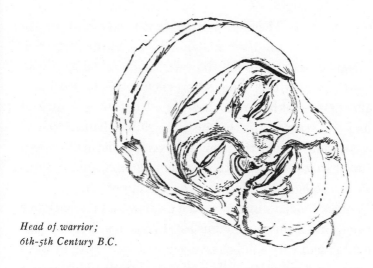

Head of warrior;
6th-5th Century B.C.

Uncle Larnth laid both hands on Vel's shoulders, and his farewell was grave and silent, man to man. Vel was moved, though he would never have admitted it. He bent over, picked up his box which the slave had set down on the ground, and, hunched from the weight of it, climbed cautiously onto the slippery gangway that reached from the deck to the shore where it had sunk into the sand. The cat followed him with dignity, but the moment he was on board he leaped down the ladder into the dark hold and vanished.

"My ship!" Vel thought proudly. On the deck of the slender bireme beside the single mast, was a kind of wooden hut with two bunks in it; astern, under the captain's bridge, were two others. The sailors slept on the upper deck, wherever they liked, or with the oarsmen. Panting, Vel flung his box down on one of the bunks, which was merely a thin mattress with an animal's skin

on top of it. Then he went back on deck and ran to
lean over the rail astern. Below him was the huge ram
designed to cut through the water and carved as a wild
boar's head with a long, sharp snout, ears folded back,
and fierce-looking eyes that glared out to sea. It still
had red stains on it, because the sailors had sacrificed
a cock and a goat the previous evening and had poured
the blood over it, chanting ancient, complicated prayers
to the gods of the deep and of the upper air.

Aules Pulena's own ship, the *Captain,* was remarkable
even for Tarquinia, the busiest Tyrrhenian port. It was
a large and very solid oak vessel, with no less than three
masts and complex sails and oars astern. This meant
two helmsmen, three tiers of oars, and altogether sixty
oarsmen. Merchant ships as a rule had only a single
mast; great skill was needed to manage the heavy three-
masted ships with their tangle of sails and to get the
oarsmen to keep time. But Aules Pulena, unlike many
merchants, refused to hand his ship over to a captain
and lie on his bunk drinking and working out his profits.
He was captain of his own ships and knew the routes of
the Great Sea as well as his helmsman Ocno.

The *Captain* drew up its dripping anchors. The clanking of chains was drowned in the shouts of the small
crowd on shore yelling greetings, warnings, and farewells. Vel saw Uncle Larnth, an imposing figure in his
purple cloak glittering with gold, waving at them. He
waved back and quickly joined Ocno astern. The helmsman had one foot set firmly on the ship's side, and one
of the stroke oars, which served as a rudder, raised; and

he was all set to bear on the other with his full weight and get the *Blue Boar* away in the wake of the *Captain*.

"We're off, we're off!" shouted Vel, leaping excitedly around the helmsman.

The *Captain* went about turning to the open sea, westward, in a wide sweep. On the mizzenmast, a small square sail was quickly hoisted to catch the wind. With a sudden heave, Ocno flung himself hard on the right oar, and the two rows of oarsmen in the ship's hold dipped their oars into the water in perfect time; they flashed in the sun again, dipped again, flashed and dipped, faster and faster, till the bireme with its boar's snout swept gracefully around to take its place in the wake of the *Captain*.

Vel drew a deep breath. He felt so happy that even Ibico seemed less tiresome than usual. In any case, Ibico or no Ibico, he was at sea in one of the two finest ships in Tarquinia, just starting on a long voyage to lands more mysterious than the island of Sicula and the shores of Ionia. And he—Vel—was practically captain. He marched slowly along the deck, straddling as he had seen sailors do.

"To Populonia!" he barked out, but in his head. "Full sail to Populonia, my hearties, by all the gods in the depths of the sea!"

For a few hours the two ships hugged the shore, driven by the oars and helped by a single sail. Then, about midday, the west wind let them hoist all the sails. Ocno made fast the stroke oars and leaped off the deck, yelling orders liberally sprinkled with oaths.

"May Poseidon swallow the lot of you before night-fall! You bunch of peasants, it's a plough and oxen you want—not a ship! Hold that mainsail! Hold it hard! Hurry! Get hold of those ropes there! Get a move on!"

But the great rectangular sail unfolded as it should, flapping and catching the wind in its folds. At first it looked like a long, bundled up intestine, then it swelled out and finally stood against the gray-blue sky in a huge white crescent. The boat creaked in every joint and seemed to bound ahead and then settle to a constant speed. The sailors wiped their brows with their cloth caps.

"Ocno, look at the *Captain*!" Vel cried.

Aules Pulena's three masts, now too far away for orders to reach the *Blue Boar*, seemed suddenly covered with white clouds, as if by magic. The sails had been only partly hoisted, in order not to leave the *Boar* too far behind, but the effect was impressive all the same.

"When you were young, weren't there ships like that?" Vel asked.

The old man shrugged gruffly.

"Give me the *Boar* any day. One sail to catch the wind, and another when it blows the other way. That's all I need!"

"But look at the way it's running!" Vel insisted. "Do look—it's so lovely!"

"Lovely, I grant you. But these newfangled ideas are all very well for youngsters. And for Greeks," he added, seeing Ibico, who had padded solemnly up to them.

"Never happy with what they've got and what they can do. Always wanting change! Why, they'd gobble up the whole world, if we gave them half a chance."

"The wolf calling the tiger violent!" sneered Ibico. "Do you call that ring in your ear a badge of peace?"

"We're sons of Ulysses, Tyrrhenian. We were crossing the seas to find new peoples and new lands when the name Etruscan didn't exist."

"Did you, now? But less than fifty springs ago we made you take your paws off the Corsicans' land. That day we cut off a fair slice of that long nose you go poking in everywhere."

But Vel broke into the quarrel, burning with curiosity.

"You never told me about the Corsicans, Ocno. Did you really fight? Leave Ibico alone and tell me about the battle."

The old helmsman looked around, still annoyed. But the ship was sailing fast, with a straight wake behind it. The sails were taut and the oars pulled up in the oarlocks, the oarsmen flung forward across them, resting. So long as the west wind blew there was nothing to be done. Vel pressed on.

"Come on, Ocno, tell me. Can't you see the *Boar* is going ahead on its own?"

They both sat down on deck, their backs resting against the cabin. Ocno's eyes were already clouded with memories, and he stared ahead as if he were gazing at things he alone could see in the distance.

"In those days I was a sailor at Cere. You've never seen a warship."

"But the *Boar* can defend itself if it has to!" said Vel. "We've got axes and spears and swords, and so has the *Captain*."

"Yes, of course. At sea you can never be sure. It's not just the fury of Poseidon and the gods under the waves, and it's not just the monsters and the currents. There are other dangers as well, dangers from men."

"You should know!" snorted Ibico.

But Ocno refused to be drawn.

"But warships, they're quite different. Mine was two-masted and narrow, half the size of this. And beside the *Captain*, why, it would have been like a puppy by its mother. But fast! And lively, as well. I wasn't a helmsman then—I was just fifteen springs and two moons old. And the captain—may Aita torment him in hell with his whip of serpents, for the wolf's soul he had!— was a god at sea. If you'd seen that ship, with its bronze covered bow and its huge beak, skimming over the water as lightly as an albatross! Well, those of us from Cere formed the right wing beside the Carthaginian fleet, our allies—huge great ships those Carthaginians had. Lined up in formation like that, we must have looked like a swarm of horseflies on the flank of an ox. But like horse-flies, we drew blood. As the Greeks found out!"

And he glared at Ibico.

"Yes, I know," said Vel. "You were in the Sardinian sea."

"Opposite the shores of Corsica. There's a Greek city there called Alalia. The Greek biremes and triremes were drawn up in a semicircle in front of the port, and the weather was so clear that we could see the soldiers with their small round shields and shining helmets very clearly on the decks of two of the ships. The Carthaginians were drawn up in the middle in a wedge shape to break through the Greek line, and we were to the right and left of them, waiting for the signal to close in and trap the two stumps of the fleet by shutting them in to stop them from getting away. That's what we had to do, see? Because our ships were so light and quick. Oh, you should have been there waiting for the Carthaginian trumpets to blow! I remember there wasn't a breath of wind, the sails were struck, and the oars raised; it wasn't easy to keep our position, I can tell you—it all fell on the helmsman. Then at last the Carthaginian flagship sounded the trumpet—I recognized it from the red mast and the silver figurehead on the stern. We saw the ships in the middle moving, slowly at first. They didn't look as if they were moving at all; then they speeded up. We followed them, our oars going in once for every two of theirs, close together but with our bows not in line—each one a few feet ahead of the one next to it."

"And what about the Greeks?" said Vel, listening with the closest attention.

"They were waiting for the attack in the same formation they'd been in all night. When we attacked it was morning, and the sun was in our favor—shining in their faces and warming our backs. Yet I was cold—by all the sea gods, I was cold. I remember I had a doublet and a pair of leather breeches made of fine, soft, strong leather

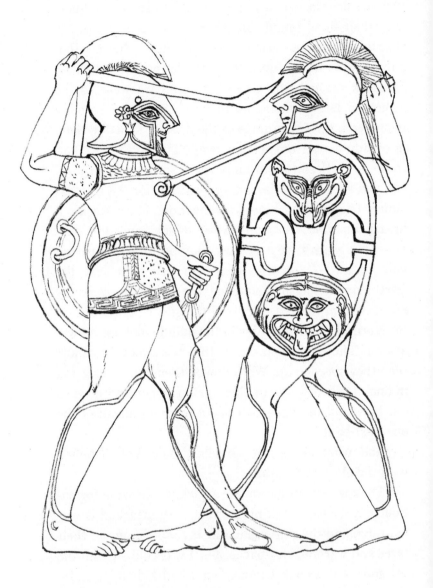

Bronze relief on a chariot; about 550 B.C.

tanned in Cere that had cost me a whole month's pay, a whole jar of wine from Campania; and I was wearing a bronze helmet. Around my neck I was wearing this."

And the old man drew up a greasy leather cord that hung around his wrinkled neck. Out came a curious talisman, hidden under his clothes. It was round and made of whitish material that looked like ivory, and in the center was a blue stone veined with black. Vel held out his hand and took it, wonderingly.

"An old woman gave it to me. She was half a witch and said she came from Umbria, but she spoke like a wild Sicilian—as if she came from the Great Island, and Turms alone knows how she ever got to Cere. But it's a powerful amulet. It cures the fevers that weaken a man and protects him from wounds. It's the eye of Uni, queen of the gods."

"But tell me about the battle," said Vel, quickly losing interest in the talisman.

"My worst time in the battle was when the Carthaginian flagship and another two met the Greeks and we were there practically still, waiting for the trumpet— two blasts that were our signal. I wasn't afraid any more, nor were the others, and, by Maris of the bronze battle-ax, how we were burning as we waited there, doing nothing while the Greek ships lay before us! And then to hear the din of battle coming clearly across the water! It lasted a long time, or so it seemed to me. I wasn't noticing the time, of course, and the deck was burning the soles of my feet. Then one of the Carthaginian ships shot two burning arrows and in a moment the sails of two Greek ships were in flames. The sailors couldn't put the fire out, of course, and the burning tow soaked in resin kept bursting out with sparks which it flung about the decks. But the wind from inland blew the smoke in our direction and pretty soon all we could see were the ships directly in front of us—we couldn't see the battle at all. But the Greeks seemed closer to us and then we realized they had gotten sick of waiting and were coming across to us. I don't know how we kept still, but remember, Vel, discipline is the first thing a soldier learns. At last we heard the trumpets sounding, and at that very moment the friendly gods of the air sent us a great puff of wind from the right that cleared the whole scene. The Carthaginians had broken the Greek line in the middle and I recognized their flagship, which had grappled with a Greek trireme, and the two of them were doing a strange dance of death on the calm sea. But I hadn't long to look. The trumpet blared a second time and the oarsmen burst out like a hurricane into a rowing rhythm I've never heard of since and no ship can keep up for more than twelve times to a hundred pulsebeats. The boatswain yelled and cursed and whipped their backs and arms like a mad man, and the ship flew over the waves."

"Did you ram the Greek ship?" asked Vel, who had leaped up with excitement.

"Not right away. Only five of our ships went toward the Greeks; mine, and another ten with it, shot off westward with all the power the oarsmen could muster,

and before the Greeks realized what had happened—
why, they moved like buffaloes in a swamp, compared
with us! We swooped down their flank and came up behind them. I was flung down on deck by the shock
when the beak of my ship burst through the side of a
Greek one and our deck tore through their upper deck
with a crash of splintering wood. Then I found myself
among my comrades on deck, hitting out hard with my
short battle spear. But I was bending over a Greek I'd
stunned and was just going to finish him off with a stab
of my knife, when a cursed cudgel gave me a glancing
blow on the head. I fell on top of the Greek and, almost
without realizing it, plunged the knife into his throat.
That was all I saw or heard."

"Was the wound very bad?"

"Well! My head's hard. The bronze helmet clanged
like a broken goblet, but it saved my life. The helmet,
and my comrades—may the gods of the underworld protect them, because they must all have made that long
journey by now. Before they shoved the Greek ship off
ours, they had carried me below, half dead."

"Did the battle go on much longer?"

"Till sunset. I hadn't recovered enough to notice. I
lay rotting in the hold all during the celebrations, and
it was only when we got back to Cere that I found we
and the Carthaginians had won and the Greeks had to
share the island with us and let our merchants have
privileged conditions and markets right in the heart of
Corsica. We made a pact of friendship with the Cartha-

ginians and neither of us has broken it since."

Ibico, who had been listening silently and angrily, now smiled ironically.

"Tyrrhenian," he said gravely, "I've listened to you and remembered things that sadden a Hellenic heart, but your last words make me smile. I know what happens when the wolf makes a pact with the sparrowhawk. The time will come when Carthage will find the Great Sea too small for the two of you, and won't let anyone establish bases—not you or anyone else."

"When that day comes, do you think the Greeks will still be remembered in the western seas?" retorted Ocno. "The power of the twelve cities extends so far over land and sea, that neither you, who've learned such a lot in those schools where they teach you to talk and nothing else, nor I, who know something of the sea and its routes, can measure even a part of it."

"Fate rules the destinies of men," retorted Ibico, clearly pleased with the way the talk was going. But Vel, who was not too interested in philosophical argument, squatted down in the bow, and, as the pair carried on a heated argument, was joined by his cat, who seemed satisfied after his survey of the hold. Ocno worked himself up into a rage, shook his head furiously, and waved his arms threateningly, while Ibico, to show how crude his opponent's tactics were, assumed a dignified pose. Vel was enjoying himself.

"I bet they'll end up hitting each other. Ibico would get the worst of it!" he thought hopefully. The argument went on and on without their coming to blows.

Finally Vel grew tired and gazed out to sea. And when he did so he thought he could see a faint bluish mark, which made the line of the horizon slightly uneven. Yes, it was—there was no doubt about it. Vel leaped to his feet.

"Land ahoy! Land to the East!"

"By Poseidon, boy!" Ocno was beside him. "Let me see. Yes, may your genius give you good eyes! It's the western headland."

Land was appearing more and more clearly to starboard. Since there was a favorable wind, the ships approached very quickly. As the *Boar* sailed majestically past the promontory, which rose steeply from the purplish-blue sea, a hilly island appeared, covered with vegetation except where bare rocks appeared, streaked with white.

"Who lives on that island, Ocno?" asked Vel, gazing at the shimmering ridge of land that seemed to be fleeing before his very eyes.

"Wild boars, wild geese, goats. There are lots of islands like it or even smaller, but no one lives on them except a few rough shepherds. Useful to get water at, some of them. But we'll get to the big island where the mines are by tomorrow, if the wind holds."

The land was already far behind them, and looked like a bank of dark clouds on the sea, when an appetizing smell of food reminded Vel that he had eaten nothing since early morning. The men were sitting or squatting in a circle on the warm planks. An earthenware pot was placed in the middle and they dipped their fingers or knives into the pot while one of the ship's boys handed each of the three most important people a rough wooden bowl. Another two or three sailors, Ocno's best men, and the boatswain in charge of the oarsmen, simply helped themselves with bits of ship's biscuit, which they first used as a plate and then ate up.

"Now this is what I really like!" sighed Vel, licking the last traces of gravy off his fingers. "It's so much nicer than at home, with couches and tables and slaves wandering up and down. And the food's a thousand times better."

"It's the sea air, boy. In this spring wind you'd eat a shark!"

At the word shark Vel's ears cocked. Ocno was going to tell another of his amazing tales, and what better end to a good meal than an adventure story. Yes, it was fine hearing the old man's voice that went so well with the splash of the waves against the keel, and it was better still if you listened with your eyes shut. Ocno looked hard at Vel as he lay on the ropes, and saw his chest rising and falling rhythmically; he stopped talking and smilingly shook his head.

"The gods of the sky and the spirits of the earth are kind to the young and generous with the gift of sleep. I must get back to my rudder."

IV.

POPULONIA, CITY OF IRON

The horizon was darkening over the last glimmers of a glorious red sunset when Vel awoke from a deep sleep. He leaped up, rubbed his aching back, and felt at once that something on board had changed. The sail was no longer hoisted and creaking above him, but he could hear the rhythmic thud of the oars. The wind had dropped and the ship was moving more slowly on a calm sea. Vel looked anxiously for the *Captain,* but it was too dark to see anything, however hard he peered. For a moment his heart contracted with fear. Had they lost their way? But just then, maybe half a mile away, he saw a gleam of flickering light and realized it was the *Captain's* night lanterns. Besides, Ocno's hoarse voice was telling the men to get their own lamps ready, and soon a large swinging oil lantern was hanging directly above the *Boar*'s head and another was hung up astern. A sailor then came near him and put a long bronze holder with a kind of cage on it in a special groove on the deck. The cage held a smoky resin torch that crackled as it burned and smelled awful. Vel hurried over to Ocno, who was at the stroke oars regulating the way they were going.

"The wind's dropped, hasn't it?"

"It has. This means we'll get there halfway through the morning instead of at dawn. But it'll start blowing again during the night, don't you worry."

"How do you know?"

"Just because, lad. Maybe I haven't read books like that tutor of yours, but this is the forty-eighth spring I've been to sea and when the wind drops before nightfall at this time of year and the dolphins come out turning somersaults, it means wind again tomorrow."

"Dolphins?" cried Vel. "Where? I've never seen any in Tarquinia, not even when we went out fishing in the big boat!"

"Look!" said Ocno, leaving the rudder and taking Vel over to the rail. In the ship's wake, lighter than the dark waves around them, shiny black creatures were playing—leaping, curving, hiding; round, snubnosed heads, sleek curved backs and crescent tails darting up playfully and vanishing again. It was an extraordinary sight, and it would hardly have seemed surprising if they had been laughing and shouting like children. Vel gazed at them, fascinated.

"Aren't they beauties! A shame I can't see them too well."

"In summer you can see them all right, in broad daylight," said Ocno. "They follow the ship and it's a bad sign when they do, because it means a storm's on its way. They're our best friends, you know, out of all the sea creatures. And that's just as it should be, because the spirit of a sailor who dies at sea lives on in every one of them."

"Oh Ocno, that's one of your stories! The soul of a sailor goes down to the kingdom of Aita, when the body grows cold and still. You know that perfectly well."

The old man shrugged.

"The laws at sea are different from the laws on land, Vel. The spirit of a sailor who dies at sea goes into a dolphin, I tell you, and when he doesn't follow in Poseidon's trail, then he goes back to help his brothers. If the man who died was a decent guy, that is. Now these were

Wall painting; 3rd-2nd Century B.C.

all good honest sailors, you see, come to tell us the wind will be back before dawn tomorrow."

After a frugal supper, there was no escape from Ibico who managed to pen Vel in the cabin for a long, dreary geometry lesson from which he escaped only when it was time to sleep.

The rhythmical squeaking of the mainsail woke him, and when he left the cabin he realized at once that Ocno had been right about the dolphins. The sail was again bellying in the west wind, which had blown away the white morning mist and made the sky very bright and clear. To port Vel could see the *Captain*'s sails, and beyond them the long low ridge of an island.

"That's the island of Etalia," said Ibico, who was standing near him, neat as ever in a spotless, uncrumpled tunic, for he undressed before going to bed, to the sailor's enormous amusement.

"I'd like to go there and see those new iron mines. I can only see the outline of the hills from here."

Ocno came over to them, straddling crab-like, as he always did. On land it looked very funny, but here on deck it seemed at one with the movement of the ship.

"There's nothing to see in the mines, lad. Only red earth and lots of black holes and a row of poor wretches —slaves and criminals burrowing like moles in the earth. We won't have anything to do with them: just load up with bronze and iron at Populonia, then sacrifice to the gods so they'll send us a good wind as far as Massalia. The mines, indeed! Sooner have two months at sea on biscuit and water without once touching land than the mines. Look! The master, he's already sailing in to land."

Vel gazed admiringly at the *Captain*'s maneuver. The great three-masted ship in full sail was tacking slowly eastward, until it gradually turned and Vel could see its full length. Ocno had rushed to the rudder and the sailors were working hard to follow in the *Captain*'s wake. For a while the two ships sailed around the shores of the great gulf before the island of Etalia. Then they turned back around the promontory that enclosed it on the North. Once they had gone past the point, the shoreline became more and more broken and indented, with small green promontories and patches of white, rushing currents, and rocks ringed with foam. The *Blue Boar* had speeded up, though the wind was no stronger. The waves started lapping the ship's narrow sides more noisily and its wake became wider and more foamy. Ocno smiled at Vel's puzzled face.

"It is a current that goes around the promontory we've just passed, and dies in the port of Populonia. You find them here, between the mainland and the island, and we've got to go around a longer way before landing. But to make up for it the current takes us there fast, and we'll gain time in the end. In any case, there's Populonia."

On top of a hill, less than two hundred yards high but rising steeply and rockily from the sea, rose wooden-roofed houses and a temple with painted plaster columns, all huddled closely together on the small space available and looking like the painted backdrop in a theater.

On the *Captain*, sailors had climbed into the rigging, and most of the sails were struck. She swept slowly, majestically, around at the foot of the hill on which, inside its inaccessible fortress walls, stood Populonia. The *Blue Boar* caught up and the two ships entered the small crescent-shaped bay almost together. On the shore, right down to the sea, stood more houses and the foundries of Populonia.

Tarquinia had only a few warehouses and huts along the shore, apart from its wharfs; but Populonia, not counting the part up on the hill, stretched along the whole shore. Vel hung over the side trying to see everything at once.

"Hey, look at all those ships! We've certainly come at the right moment! Ocno, where's that one from?"

A long trireme with a gleaming figurehead and brightly painted sails swayed gently on the water, larger and more imposing than the other three ships—obviously Etruscan—anchored near her. Astern was an enormous bull's head, with flaring nostrils and huge painted eyes, and a bronze disc between its horns. A long handled mallet hanging on one of the horns showed that it was a gong used to give orders to the sailors—an eastern custom, as Vel knew. Slender, dark-skinned men were working hard at a huge mound of bales of something soft and light. They wore loincloths and striped caps that covered their foreheads and had symmetrical panels at the sides, falling onto their shoulders. Some of them stopped to stare curiously at the *Captain* and the *Boar* gliding into port on a single tier of oars, while the great anchors already swung against their sides.

Ocno took off his cap and waved it at the sailors, yelling something in a language that was strange to Vel. The sailors burst out laughing and shouted something back. A boy, who looked about Vel's age, appeared at the ship's side and waved at him. Vel smiled back and greeted him, first in Etruscan, then in Greek.

"Where are you from?" he asked. "Who are you? Do you understand me?"

The boy laughed and shouted *"Caire!"* which was the Greek form of greeting. His accent was odd, and it was clearly all he could say.

"Carthaginians who have come from Sicily," Ocno told him from the deck. "They've got a cargo of cotton and landed here yesterday."

"But is that damned Greek of yours still snoring like a hog? Hasn't he realized we've arrived yet?" Then he hung over the side to roar at a boat darting around the ship's keel and threatening to crash into the great stroke oars. Ocno's language could take him anywhere in the Great Sea. The boat was handled by eight strong slaves, and over it was an elaborate umbrella with an ivory handle and a silver fringe. Under this sat a man in a loose painted robe, looking very grave and gazing about him with studied indifference. He wore big gold bracelets and around his pudgy neck a collar of pure gold; it was plain that, under his billowing garments, he was

Bronze statue of youth;
5th Century B.C.

nobly fat, which meant he was someone of importance; and his skin was shiny with scented oil, another sign of his grandeur.

After peering down more closely, Ocno abruptly stopped his flow of insults, handed the rudder over to Vipis, and ran to the ship's side. He whisked off his cap and started bowing deferentially in the direction of the unresponsive umbrella, whispering information to Vel and orders to the boatswain as he did so.

"Quick work by the vultures today! It's the customs' chief come to tax us for coming into port! Down with the ladder at once. Sir, we're doing our best, please don't be impatient! My master, the noble Pulena, has told me to show you the cargo and pay the tribute in first class goods, whichever you like to choose. Here, you damned sea slugs, hurry up with the ladder!"

The ladder was thrown overboard and held tightly by one of the slaves in the boat, while the dignified character climbed up quite nimbly. Once on deck he acknowledged Ocno's bow briefly, glanced absently at Vel, and made for the hold, followed by Ocno, Vel, and a respectful scribe carrying a box full of parchment rolls. Then he started speaking in clear Etruscan, but with an accent quite unlike that of Tarquinia.

"For the ship of noble Pulena, whom you represent, a bireme cargo vessel, no doubt loaded with valuable goods, you will pay two bolts of linen, two jars of wine, and—" he gave a quick glance around—"a vase of Volterran alabaster with unguent in it."

Stunned by this exorbitant demand, Vel was just going to protest when Ocno broke in with a flood of words.

"Why sir, that's impossible! My master will never believe that noble Populonia's asking a wretched bireme for a tax like that! He'll have me whipped, thinking I've taken his goods and then invented some mean little lie to get away with it. Our cargo is pretty worthless stuff, sir: a bit of wine, poor quality at that, a few pairs of slaves' sandals, twelve bolts of cheap cloth made of linen waste, and a few pots of unguent!"

"May the gods protect us, and Turms, the god of trading, in particular!" thought Vel, astounded at Ocno's nerve. "The fellow can't possibly believe a pack of lies like that!"

But Ocno turned to a bundle in a corner and produced a few pairs of sandals which Aules Pulena intended throwing in as an extra, as was the custom if the business was satisfactorily concluded.

"As you can see, sir, it's all cheap stuff—and it's all

the same. Apart from . . . oh yes, here's something worthy of a man of taste."

And from the heap of sandals he took out a very fine leather belt, dyed purple, with chased gold buttons on it and a fringe of tiny silver leaves.

Ocno looked at it, then shook his head and stuck out his lip in a grimace.

"This certainly won't do for the merchants of Massalia, who'll sell the bronze and iron we've come to get in your beautiful city to a horde of barbarians with red pigtails. I'm sure my master didn't mean this masterpiece to go to some dirty barbarian chief. He'll be delighted if you'll accept it, sir, as a token of the Tarquinians' skill in working with gold."

The man looked at the belt and after a moment's hesitation took it, tucked it into the folds of his robe, and without a word went up the ladder and onto the deck.

"You haven't got much, I can see. Let me have a jar of wine and half a bolt of your best linen."

Ocno bowed deeply, praised the just laws of wise Populonia, yelled orders to the boatswain, and in a few minutes the boat with its colored umbrella started back again.

Ocno winked at the astonished Vel.

"Surprised, my lamb? If you learn to know the sea and its cities, you'll learn more about men in a few moons than that tame Greek owl of yours could teach you out of a hundred books."

Vel nodded and winked back.

"Why Ocno, you were clever! You were like a real
merchant, even though you're a sailor, and my father
will be grateful to you. I think we'll do good business
in Populonia—it's started well, anyhow. Isn't it smoky,
though? And ugly?"

Into the fresh morning air columns of thick smoke
rose; sometimes it was almost white, sometimes very
dark, depending on whether it came from the smelting
ovens or from the workshops where the metal was made
into thin sheets. A hundred of these were working copper and tin from the mines of Tolfa and other Etruscan
towns inland, and iron from the island of Elba, which
the Greeks called Etalia. The lower part of the town
looked sad and stuffy, but when Vel at last found himself on the wharf, followed by Ibico, the noise and excitement and variety of the swarming crowd delighted
and amused him. Even the hammers pounding the anvils, the creaking winches, and the puffing bellows that
all together sounded like a hoarse, powerful breath coming from the workshops, seemed to him gay and lively,
and he forgot the smoky sky and dirty sea and looked
longingly about him. But Ocno was burning to tell his
master how cunning and successful he had been in dealing with the customs' man, so he pushed his way through
the crowd to where the *Captain*'s boat had landed. The
harbor was not deep, and only the fishermen's boats
fringed the shore with a restless, brightly-colored border; the flat-bottomed boats loaded with ore had been
pushed up clumsily on the beach.

Aules Pulena smiled at Vel and was pleased with

Ocno's account of what had happened. But he was obviously distracted, and his eyes kept peering through the crowd looking for someone. Suddenly he stopped worrying. A servant, whose clothes and beard showed he was Greek, was walking over to them. No ordinary slave, but some kind of steward, he was carrying a register and a large abacus, and he bowed low to Aules Pulena.

"The gods of the seas and the winds have favored your sails, sir. We did not expect you early in the spring, but much later. My master, the noble Velthur Tulumnes, will be all the more happy to see you."

"We need a great deal of metal, both crude and smelted," said Aules Pulena. "Your master is sure to have bronze and iron, for I have heard that they keep finding large new deposits and that even the tips of your lances and helmets are of iron. Am I not right?"

"As far as I can judge, the noble Pulena has been rightly informed," the steward replied, his cunning little eyes gleaming. "But my master will be able to answer your questions much better than I can. He is not at the harbor today," he continued, foreseeing Aules Pulena's question. "This evening the spring celebration in honor of the goddess Turan will begin, and my master is busy with the priests in the temple preparing for them."

"So I have hardly come at the right moment," said Aules regretfully.

"Why, sir," protested the Greek. "When I was told your ships had arrived I sent a slave straight off to my master's house, and if you and those with you will deign to come in the carriage that should . . . Why, here it is!" And indeed a carriage drawn by two mettlesome horses was clattering up from the steep winding road up the hill and stopping outside a smoke-blackened building with two puffing chimneys.

Vel, who until then had been standing politely aside under his tutor's severe, watchful eye, now started scuffing the ground restlessly with his foot and finally gave the hem of his father's cloak a small tug.

"What is it, my boy?" said Aules, while the steward shouted loudly to the driver of the carriage telling him to come over.

"Father," said Vel, sounding virtuous, "if our host's busy, couldn't we have a look at his workshop before we go up to the house? That way he would have time to finish with his duties and . . ."

"And you'd satisfy your curiosity? If I'm not mistaken you've been peering at those chimneys for quite a time!"

"No, what I meant was, we could see how it's done a bit."

Aules Pulena laughed, half teasing his son, and half pleased with him.

"Hey," he called to the steward, "My son wants to see where the goods you're selling us come from and if you do any cheating over your bronze and iron!"

The Greek tittered obsequiously.

"The lion's cub must learn to kill while he's young, the merchant's son to observe and value, noble Pulena," he said. "I shall be delighted to accompany you and your son. You will see some things unknown at Tarquinia. These are two of my master's foundries, though not the largest. Boats come from the island loaded with ore which the gods enriched for our benefit, and the carts unload it here."

While he was talking, he led them into a large courtyard outside the low building with cylindrical chimneys rising from its roof. The courtyard was cluttered with hematite, the reddish mineral which was rich in iron, and darker slag, clearly ready to be carted off.

"This is what's left after the red mineral has been smelted. We throw the slag away along the seashore, where the old city once stood, so that we now have a new city built on the old, as my master says, and, thanks to this precious red stone, we shall become ever greater."

At the entrance to the huge workshop, which was half filled by the furnaces, he had to stop talking, for the noise of the great hammers beating the iron into thin sheets was deafening. But Vel rushed over to the great pot-bellied black furnaces. In one of them, which was in use, he could hear the fire roaring in its capacious belly of fireproof clay. The steward stopped the hammers for a moment and with hasty gestures explained that layers of ore alternated in the furnaces with layers of coal and wood. Shut up inside with a good draft coming through vents, the fire got the mineral up to extremely high temperatures.

"The melting takes days and at night the sky is red with burning vapors and clouds of sparks flying up out of the chimneys," the Greek continued, his flowery

Hellenic way of speaking coming through the Etruscan of Populonia. "Then an incandescent stream of metal flows from this opening into the earthenware channels waiting for it. But it's still mixed with slag, and before it becomes solid, like this, it has to be purified." With an effort he raised the end of a bar, then dropped it; the iron clanged on the stone floor.

"But this stuff isn't as strong as bronze, is it?" said Aules Pulena.

"No, but it can be made into all kinds of shapes and it's excellent for weapons, because it's easy to give it a sharp cutting edge—it makes fine razors, for instance. In a few years there will be many more furnaces and workshops in Populonia, and my guess is that iron will take over from bronze entirely."

The hammers started beating on the anvils again with a reverberating din. Vel went over to one of them, on which a bar was being flattened. An enormous charcoal burner burned at an almost unbearable heat inside it, and slaves with a mere rag for a loincloth held bars plunging into it with long forceps. Sweat streamed down their bare backs and their blackened faces seemed to Vel like the faces of grinning evil spirits; their eyes flashing red, their teeth strangely white in all that blackness. He noticed a boy of about his own age hanging onto a rope with his full weight, yet sometimes touching the ground and sometimes pulling up into the air, kicking out weirdly. The rope was tied to the top part of what seemed to be an enormous leather bellows; a great whistling hiss came from its mouth, which narrowed into a funnel, and the embers in the forge blazed up. Other slaves pulled at the ropes that raised the hammer, lifting it with the strength of their muscles, then letting it drop, and sparks rained brightly through the sooty gloom of the workshop. At every blow Vel started, yet he was fascinated by the blinding sparks and could have watched forever. But the steward suddenly came over, seized him by the arm and dragged him away from the forge, shaking his head to make him realize through the din that it was dangerous to stand so near it. At that moment there was a terrible scream and one of the slaves working at the hammer dropped the rope and put his hands to his face rolling on the floor in a frenzy. Work stopped at once, and in the sudden silence the injured man's screams were agonizing. Vel was dragged outside by his father's strong arm and saw Ibico's dead white face distorted with horror. The steward joined them, wiping his brow with a piece of his tunic.

"One of the very best slaves! That damnable splinter will blind him, as Sisimbra, another first-rate workman, was blinded less than two months back. The master will be in despair."

Vel shuddered, still shaken by the accident.

"I wouldn't live in that dark cave for anything on earth," he said. "Give me the sea and our ships any day! How can a man knuckle down to work like that, with the fear of being maimed or killed at any moment! And how can he go back to work when he's seen the other chap fall down beside him!"

But Aules Pulena interrupted him.

"You're talking like a child, Vel. Haven't your uncle and I and all the Pulenas risked for generations, our lives at sea from the days long ago when ships were just flat-bottomed boats without mast or sail? A merchant's life is as risky as that of an iron worker or a miner. It's time for us to be getting off to the house of Velthur Tulumnes."

His father's little speech sounded more or less like a rebuff, and Vel hurried into the carriage beside him without replying. Aules wanted to leave the steward behind and the man was quite ready to go back to the workshop and attend to things there. The coachman could perfectly well take them into the house. Ibico stood beside the slave, who waved the long whip of plaited leather and urged the horses on. As the carriage, with its four wheels reinforced with bronze, clattered off, they heard the sound of hammer blows, which had started started up again, coming from the workshop.

The journey up to the top of the hill was slow but short. Ibico was silent because it would have been below his dignity to speak to a lowly slave like the coachman. Aules seemed to be working things out and Vel kept fidgeting about on the seat. Sometimes he looked at the road they had already covered, the sea growing further away below them and the houses and workshops all growing smaller and smaller, and sometimes he looked at the rock and the green-girt houses that overhung the port.

V.

THE MERCHANT

The house of Velthur Tulumnes was like the finest houses in Tarquinia, but it had a very large, splendid garden surrounding it as well. The varying levels of the land had been used to make terraces on which all kinds of flowers were now blooming, and the path leading to the entrance went through a small orchard in which the trees were all in blossom, with bees buzzing noisily among them.

Outside the front door the owner of the house was just getting down from a light two-wheeled carriage, elegantly designed, its dark wood decorated with gilding. Vel was surprised at his host's small, portly figure. Velthur Tulumnes was a passionate admirer of Greek civilization, and the great riches earned by his mines and workshops were mostly spent on importing things from Greece—clothes, household objects, slaves, valuable works of art, all in large quantities. Everything in his house had to be Greek—both in the way it was furnished and in its domestic arrangements. In spite of his rather undistinguished figure, he wore a long beard, and, instead of the short tunic and large painted Etruscan *tèbennos,* a tunic that reached to his feet and a kind of long scarf draped around his shoulders and waist. His thick gray hair was not carefully plaited, as Aules Pulena's was, but cut short, which Vel thought made a very funny contrast with his bushy beard.

"His barber slipped up and shaved his head instead of his face," he thought.

The little man heard the sound of the carriage, and turning excitedly, went up to his guests.

Aules and Vel were overwhelmed by a wave of exclamations and an uninterrupted flow of friendly greetings.

"Aules Pulena! Is it really you, my friend? *Caire! Caire!*" Velthur Tulumnes cried, bounding around his tall guest who had no chance of answering a single one of his questions. "The gods were propitious, I see! You're some weeks earlier than you were last year. Poseidon's been kind this spring, and that's a fact. In any case, you know I'm not a seagull like you. I simply can't bear sailing, myself. Give me my dark mines and my home—I'm a country person, you see, not a sailor."

"Well, here's someone who doesn't agree with you," said Aules, just managing to break in. "This is my son— you'll be dealing with him soon, I expect, when the sea has rattled my bones too much and the brine has eaten up my carcass."

"Why, you're joking, my friend! The shade hasn't spun away half your life yet, and you're calling yourself old. But you're wise to think of your successor! So this is the young Pulena. Well, well! I'd love to have my sons here to help and cheer me. But they're both in Athens, alas, as pupils of the great philosopher Teognides, and it will be many moons before I see them again."

The merchant's eyes gleamed and belied his regretful tone. He was immensely proud of being able to afford the vast expense of sending his sons to study in Greece, "mother of wisdom and mistress of civilization," as he liked to put it. Aules smiled.

"You're wise to send the young Tulumnes to the holy city of Athens, my friend. They will learn wisdom there. But I prefer our own way myself, as you know, and I've got this Corinthian slave to see to Vel's education."

Hearing himself mentioned, Ibico bowed and Velthur turned to him at once, chatting fluently and enthusiastically in very correct Greek and treating him almost as amiably as if he were a guest. Then suddenly he remembered where he was, and slapped his head.

"The gods of sacred hospitality forgive me!" he exclaimed. "I'm stupider than my dwarf Arniza, keeping my guests in the garden when they're hot and tired. Forgive me, Aules, and come in, come in! You must rest after your journey and refresh yourselves with some fruit and a little wine. Here we eat at sunset, you know, in the Greek style." And he entered the pillared hall, clapping his hands and calling the slaves who came running in. Somewhat bewildered by all his host's chatter, Vel followed his father and Ibico into the house.

"We saw your steward at the port," Aules managed to say, "and he warned us you'd be kept busy today, and for three more days, with grave and important duties."

"Yes, I'm afraid so. A poor merchant already weighed down with work and responsibility really shouldn't have them thrust on him," said Velthur, with such fake modesty that even Vel smiled. "But it seems my help is needed in dealing with some very serious matters. You sailors are lucky, you know—you'll be here for the feast of the goddess Turan, whom I prefer to honor as Aphrodite. And wasn't the goddess born of the sea? So she'll protect you on your journey, which I'm sure doesn't end here. I know the Pulenas too well, and I've heard of a great new ship which you brought into the harbor, with no less than three masts."

"Your ears and eyes are everywhere, so they tell me; in fact I believe you've got a hundred of them, like the Greek monster Argos," said Aules with a sly smile.

Velthur burst out laughing, and slapped him on the arm.

"Why, that Greek tutor of yours hasn't just been teaching your son, I see! A hundred eyes like Argos, that's rich! But we'll talk business later, and hear about your journeys; meantime, I hope you'll find your rooms comfortable."

There were a great many finely decorated rooms. Vel was given an inner one with his tutor, while Aules was honored with the largest in the house, which opened onto the courtyard. Father and son had a quick meal in their rooms. The main meal was to come later. Then Vel slept for a while, but when he woke the sun was still high, and Ibico was fast asleep breathing heavily, as a weary adult does. Vel, who had flung himself onto the luxurious couch after taking off his sandals, went over to his sailor's box for a look, and found some short tunics and another pair of sandals, much finer than those he had worn on the journey, a heavy cloak carefully folded, and the small embroidered purse with the silver didrachmas in it. These reminded him of his mother, and his heart swelled with homesickness.

"Tomorrow I'll ask Velthur where I can buy a fine present for Mother," he thought. "There must be a market in Populonia. I'll buy her a new buckle for her purple dress embroidered with gold. And now I'd better get changed; they seem terribly formal in this house."

In the corner of the room there was a copper urn standing on slender legs, and, moving very carefully to avoid waking Ibico, Vel poured some water into it from the jug and washed his face and arms. Then he put on his best clothes and the soft leather sandals embroidered with silver thread that reached his calves. He even thought of wearing the cloak—which was something

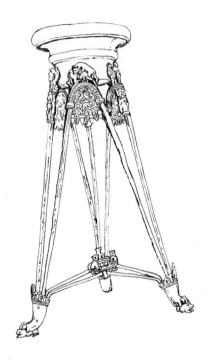

Vulcan-type bronze tripod;
6th Century B.C.

grown men wore—but was afraid of looking ridiculous.
After listening suspiciously to Ibico's breathing for a
moment, he slipped out of the room.

The garden was beautiful in the sunshine, and Vel
wandered along the paths between the plants and grass
until he reached a well-cut lawn, with a fountain and
a statue in the middle of it. A mischievous face above a
goatee beard seemed to be winking at him. It had pointed
ears and a pair of little horns among the curls on its
head. "Why, it's the god Pan!" Vel exclaimed, surprised.

He went over to the fountain. The statue was of
weather-stained white marble, rather clumsy looking but
with a highly expressive face that looked as if it was

longing to speak. It was quite unlike the faces of the wooden statues Vel had so often seen at the temple at Tarquinia. Those statues at home were motionless and severe, with staring, wide-open eyes and a terrible smile that made them infinitely remote from human beings. But this one made Vel feel quite at home; in fact it seemed perfectly natural to put out a hand and touch the pointed ear, which reminded him of some small wild creature.

Wham! Something light and dry hit him on the neck. Vel spun around, a little startled. Someone giggled gaily in a clump of reeds at his left.

The reeds rustled, as if moved by a breath of wind; Vel leaped forward to see who was teasing him, and nearly landed in a deep fish-pond half covered in water weeds. Two large white birds, unlike any he had ever seen, moved slowly and disdainfully away, curving their long necks; and it looked as if there were no other living things nearby. Vel knew someone was watching him from a bush but he pretended not to notice it; he shrugged and began collecting pebbles to throw into the greenish pond water. Suddenly, out of the corner of his eye, he caught a glimpse of something white behind the large flowering oleander on his left. Without appearing to search, he went over in that direction, and, when he was near the bush, suddenly whirled around and was beside it in a couple of leaps. A girl of about his own age was crouching on the ground. Although she pretended to be scared, her black eyes gleamed with fun and Vel knew he had not scared her in the least.

"What are you doing here?" he asked.

The girl burst out laughing.

"This is *my* garden. I might ask you what you're doing here. But I know. You're the son of the merchant from Tarquinia, and you came this morning with your father and two ships: one was huge and everyone's talking about it, and the other was smaller. That's right, isn't it? You've come to buy iron from my father, but you won't be leaving for a couple of days because they're having the solemn feasts of the goddess Turan."

"It's all quite true," answered Vel, surprised. "But how do you know so much? I've never seen you in the house. In fact I don't think I've seen any woman who wasn't a slave. Sorry if I jumped on you like that. I thought Velthur Tulumnes had only two sons."

The girl shrugged.

"You don't know my father. He loves Greece and he says Greek ways are the wisest and most civilized in the world, especially the ways of Athens: so we live in the Athenian way. I have a Greek governess and she says that in Athens the women always have to stay in a hidden part of the house and never show themselves to the men. That's why you didn't see me this morning. My mother and I won't even come to the banquet. But I heard all about you from the slaves, even before the carriage came through the gate."

"Now I see why you're dressed like that. I thought it was the fashion in Populonia."

"Do you mean I look funny, dressed like this?"

"Oh no, no!" Vel said hastily, alarmed at the idea

of angering her. "Not at all—on the contrary—you're very, very pretty. But if your governess is always after you," he went on, trying to change the subject, "how have you managed to come here alone?"

"I'm not really alone. I sent Aglaia to get my work and she'll soon be here. So I must say goodbye!"

And she peered around uneasily.

"Wait, no one's around yet," said Vel.

He liked her. She was so pretty and polite, though different from the girls in Tarquinia he had so often played and quarreled with.

"Tomorrow there'll be the games in honor of the goddess. My father's very pious and he's one of the magistrates in charge of the games, so my mother and I'll be there in the theater. You'll see me in the covered gallery. *Caire!*"

"What's your name?" Vel cried. But the girl was already running toward the house.

Vel went on walking around the garden, thinking over what the girl had told him. How strange that people's customs varied so much! His mother had always seemed to him the most important person at home, just as his father was in charge when it came to ships and warehouses and stores in the small dockyard. Naturally neither his mother nor even his aunt Hermia, Uncle Larnth's easy-going wife, would ever have taken part in "men's business." But the house of Velthur Tulumnes seemed to him dreary and dull in spite of all its luxury, without friendly, courteous women to make things pleasant and attractive to a guest.

"I'll have a good look at the covered gallery tomorrow," he thought. "Let's hope the games are as fine as they say. I wonder if there'll be chariot races!" And at the thought of this, the girl in Greek costume went out of his mind entirely. It was two years since Vel had been allowed to attend the chariot races, which the Tarquinians were so passionately fond of. Splendid horses were kept in the great grasslands that stretched between Tarquinia and Tuscany, and a cavalry corps, composed of youngsters from the noblest and richest families, had been established in the army. When the games were held the entire town was involved, and the excitement was enormous. Anyone who could afford to bet did so and people sometimes risked everything they owned. The winner of the races was honored as a hero, almost a god.

Vel found his father and his host talking cordially. Velthur was showing his guest the complicated hydraulic plant that he had installed to bring water to his garden and the house.

"I see, Velthur," said Aules, nodding gravely. "Our town is built on a pretty high hill as well, so we have a serious problem too. The *aquilices*—and as you know, they're the best in Etruria—have searched vainly with their magic rods, and all we can do is collect what the gods of the sky send when they're merciful and keep it in deep tanks. But Fortune has smiled on you."

"She has—the nymphs of the spring have favored me. A fountain comes from the wood behind the house, and, as you see, it's controlled and directed by a great many culverts and comes spurting out of jets. The women of the house throw crowns of flowers into its basin and make offerings to the divinity that smiles from its depths. And I tell you,"—Velthur added, lowering his voice mysteriously—"because you're a friend, that I've seen the nymph myself."

Aules looked at him with a smile, but Velthur seized his arm and, coming close to his ear, murmured, "It was one afternoon, in the middle of summer, when I'd gone to the woods to rest by the spring. There I had a marvelous dream in which the sacred winged goddesses that accompany the spirits to the kingdom of Aita appeared to me; and then, when I woke up, I saw, I swear to you, I saw a very beautiful pale face in the depths of the shell of water among the swaying plants. It was the face of a goddess, of a winged spirit."

Vel listened wide-eyed. What Velthur said came as no surprise, since everything in a man's life, from the moment he was born to the moment he must leave on the mysterious one-way journey, was interwoven with the divine. The great gods who thundered in the sky and the lesser gods who lived under the earth were always at man's back, judging and arranging his life, speaking to him through a thousand signs and through the augurs and soothsayers.

"It must be true," replied Aules Pulena. "The gods must have visited you because you honor their holy name with your feasts and are concerned in their worship . . . It is a sign of quite remarkable good will to let a traveler on earth see the divine face."

The two men were silent and walked on thoughtfully,

and Vel was proud to have shared in such serious talk. But the light city carriage with its wheels ornamented with gold was standing outside the house, and at once Velthur shook off his pensiveness and became the shrewd merchant with an eye to his own interests.

"If you're ready to show me your goods, Aules, the carriage will take us down to the harbor," he said. "Tomorrow morning you can have them taken to my warehouses and so have the ships empty for the cargo of metal. As soon as half the sun's course is done, we cannot talk business, because the games will be waiting for us at the theater."

For the rest of the afternoon Vel followed the two men, first onto the *Boar*, then onto the *Captain*. Velthur Tulumnes wisely kept quiet or else shook his head regretfully, as he looked at the pieces of linen, one after another, and twirled around the beautiful sandals made by the artisans of Tarquinia. Two alabaster perfume jars from Volterra were carefully sealed with beeswax. Velthur broke the seals, took off the lids, and sniffed ecstatically at the exquisite scent. The *Boar*'s cargo was quickly examined, and then the three of them went onto the *Captain*, which lay rocking gently on the sparkling sea, its sails struck and stoutly bound by the shrouds. Velthur admired its fine proportions, its brave, dashing air, its three masts: no three-masted ship had yet been seen at Populonia, only the ordinary two- or single-masted cargo ships. Even the Carthaginians, whose fleet everyone thought the most powerful in the Great Sea, had very few ships as splendid.

But Aules was waiting in the narrow passage for Velthur to come out of the hold. The *Captain* carried fabrics and leather goods too and fifty large terra-cotta jars sealed and filled with delicious, slightly resinous wine from the vineyards inland behind Tarquinia. When Velthur had finished dictating to his steward the list of goods he wanted, Aules led him, as if by chance, to a small door. This led to a small space deep in the hold.

"My friend, I've got something to show you," he said. "I hadn't really meant these for you, but I know how artistic you are and I'd like you to see a collection that's really quite special."

From the wooden wall he took a lamp hung on a long copper chain, with three jets. Vel was sent running to light it from the fire always kept going on deck in a big earthenware pot covered with ashes. He went as fast as he could because he was burning with curiosity: whatever was there in the secret room down in the hold? Something very valuable, that was obvious. But he had no idea what it could be. He had seen nothing special brought aboard, and he thought he had been pretty observant at Tarquinia about what was going on. The bright glow of the lantern lit Aules up as he solemnly drew the complicated bolts; the little door creaked slowly open. Vel sighed with disappointment, but Velthur Tulumnes looked as if he was carried away in some glorious dream. Fastened firmly by bronze brackets to small wooden pillars fixed in the floor, were five large Attic vases: two amphoras, two large goblets, and a three-handled water jug. The shining pottery was deco-

rated all over with red figures of gods and heroes—
processions of the god Bacchus, with satyrs wearing
crowns of vine leaves, Apollo playing his lyre, and the
battle of heroes and Amazons. All these were shown
with an astonishing grace, confidence and expressive-
ness.

Trembling with emotion, Velthur Tulumnes looked
at one of the goblets which showed Achilles killing the
Trojan prisoners. In the wavering light of the three
oil-fed jets which highlighted and shadowed the figures,
they looked as if they were moving. Velthur put out his
hand, but without daring to touch the goblet. He simply
followed the lines of the figures with his finger in the
air. Some of them resigned and submissive, some threatening and vindictive. He was smiling almost sadly; and
at last he came to himself again and turned to Aules,
speaking in an odd, angry way.

"For these—all five of them, mind you—you can have
the entire metal cargo of the *Boar*. The other goods will
be enough for you to exchange and fill up the *Captain*—
no more and you know it. Top quality bronze and iron,
and weapons you can choose yourself."

Aules shook his head.

"I've got to take these vases to Massalia. Cele Aulenna
wants them for some noble Greek house, I don't know
which, but he's ordered them. I got them from Athens
last autumn with one of the last cargoes that came in
before the winter storms. Do you see the figures? There
aren't many with red figures yet. I've only got black
figures on mine, done by the old method of decorating

Attic pottery. But the modern Athenian artists have invented a new way, it seems, and it does away with all
the old rules. I like them much better like this, though—
the new figures look alive, don't you think so?"

"They're marvelous, Aules. You know how I love
these wonderful Greek things. There are workshops of
craftsmen in Populonia copying the forms and colors
from Greek models, but their vases are as different from
the originals as the sun in winter is from the sun in
spring. These vases must be mine, Aules. I'll adorn my
house with them and when the gods say it is my last day,
I'll take them with me on my journey to Aita."

Aules pondered awhile, stroking the edge of his tunic
and frowning. At last he said, "I've got a suggestion to
make to you, and maybe we'll come to some agreement.
But it's delicate and private. We'll discuss it at your
house, if you will."

"Very well. And now I think we've finished, haven't
we? I'm sure you kept these marvels to the end on
purpose. You knew perfectly well I couldn't resist them."
And Velthur clapped his hand on Aules' shoulder,
laughing without rancor; in fact he recognized Pulena's
skill in trading, and admired and respected him for it.

The sun was setting when they left the ships. The
last flat-bottomed transport boats and fishing boats
that had gone out that morning before daylight were
hurrying back. The glowing evening star, which sailors
love, was shining steadily in the transparent blue sky.

Velthur Tulumnes' banquet was extremely lively. He
was a generous patron and the best artists in Populonia

were delighted to come to his rich table. But the place of honor was given to Zilc, the most important of the city's officials, and a friend of Velthur's. Vel, being the youngest, was relegated to a lowly place beside his tutor. Ibico seemed delighted with the Tulumnes household. He had already become friendly with the steward, a Greek whose father had emigrated to Sicily and had served Tulumnes so well that he had earned the position of freedman.

They were discussing the political situation in Greece, when the musicians stopped, and Velthur Tulumnes rose on his cushions holding up a goblet.

"My friends, I propose a toast to the success of my friend Aules Pulena, a brave and able merchant, on his journey. May the gods go with him and his son as far as Massalia, and may Poseidon and our venerable Turan, whom the Greeks call Aphrodite, go with them in particular. Come, let us pour libations to the god of salt water, and the sea goddess, the splendid Turan–Aphrodite!"

As everyone acclaimed the toast, the great hall, with its tall columns and circular beamed roof, rang with voices and laughter. Vel hoped Ibico and the steward would go on talking. Young though he was, he was thoughtful, and shared his tutor's passionate defense of Greece, a small, brave country, in its longing for freedom as it faced the unlimited might of the Persians. But serious political talk was over. Slaves hurriedly cleared away the remains of the food and left only the tablecloths and the goblets, which were constantly refilled, on the low tables. From wreaths of flowers encircling the columns and lamps and hanging in garlands on the walls, came the sweet scent of dying petals. A group of dancers came in and arranged themselves in the space between the tables—they were girls and boys wearing thin eastern veils with gold ornaments at their wrists and ankles, and their hair oiled, scented, and tied with ribbons of pure gold. Vel had never seen such a large, richly dressed troupe, in which Greek beauty was combined with Etruscan luxury. Like the adults around him, and

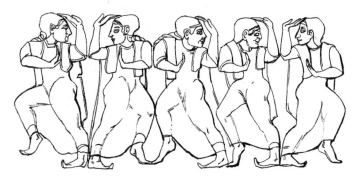

From a relief on an urn; 6th Century B.C.

encouraged by his own generous Etruscan temperament, he gave himself up entirely to the pleasure of watching the dancers and listening to the music.

"What lucky people we are," he thought, "and how the gods must love us! Where else in the world do people live as well as we do and see the fine things that we see?" This was his last thought before he fell asleep on the soft mattress, while all around him others—including the dignified Zilc—were lying on their couches or even on the floor, clothes all rumpled, blind drunk.

Late the next morning Vel awoke. His mouth was bitter, his tongue sour, and he felt very depressed. He sat up on the edge of the bed, legs dangling, eyes scarcely able to open. Ibico was not there and the sun was already high.

"There's an evil spirit running around my head," he grumbled, "and it's filled my legs with cotton wool." He felt terrible and rather ashamed of what had happened, even a little frightened, and tried to cheer himself with the thought of what he would tell Ocno about his drinking adventure—then he decided to say nothing about its effect. As he was rubbing his aching stomach, a wrinkled old slave with motherly eyes came into the room carrying some steaming linen cloths, a basin that smelled strongly of vinegar, and a bowl full of some dark liquid. Vel sighed, remembering wistfully how often old Ninia or his mother had come into his room carrying similar remedies and had firmly cured any ailments too small to need a doctor. It never occurred to him to refuse when the slave put him back to bed with a hot cloth on his forehead, and he gulped down what was in the bowl without stopping for breath. The drink tasted disgusting, but after less than ten minutes Vel felt a great deal better. He had regained strength in his legs and the band around his head seemed to have melted away. He smiled at the woman and thanked her.

"You shouldn't thank poor Zila, young sir," she answered in Etruscan, with a thick country accent. "If my little mistress hadn't told me to come I wouldn't be here."

Vel leaped out of bed, flinging the cloth off his forehead.

"Your little mistress? Do you mean the lady of the
house?"

"Oh no! The young lady, my little Seia. She called
me this morning and said, 'Nurse, look after the Tarquinian merchant's son the way you do when the god
Fufluns has been generous.' Ah, Fufluns is a powerful
god, especially when he inflames young heads! And my
darling was right, wasn't she? Oh, she's wise, you
know, though she's so young. But you haven't met her
yet, have you? Why, she's as sweet and as pretty as
one of Turan's handmaidens."

Vel shrugged, annoyed by the old woman's teasing.

"No, I've never met a wise, pretty girl like that! But
tell your young mistress I don't need these rags of yours
or this revolting medicine, do you hear? It's sourer than
sea water. I'm perfectly well and all I want is to join my
father down at the harbor."

Seia's nurse (come to think of it, it wasn't a bad
name, Seia—and he was glad he knew it!) quite unruffled by this outburst, withdrew with a bow and a few
more teasing chuckles. But Vel at once realized he had
no wish to go down to the harbor; his father had gone
there with Velthur Tulumnes and—better still—with
Ibico. He searched the garden in vain, but he had to con-
tent himself with watching from a raised lookout, the
movement of boats and the men swarming on the ships.

But the sight did not hold him for long. As always his
thoughts ran to the sea and to the *Boar,* which was now

his very own ship; Vel considered it as if it were entrusted entirely to him, for the faithful Ocno was hardly
a Pulena himself. Throughout the morning, while he was
waiting for his father and his host, he thought about the
unknown part of the journey that lay ahead, and of
distant Massalia where the West came to an end, and
which few Etruscan merchants, even the ablest, had
ever visited. Had he not been so tired he would have
gone down to check the loading of the cargo; but he
hated the thought of Ocno and the sailors seeing him as
he had seen himself in the fishpond, with yellow face and
rings around his eyes. How they would have laughed!
And a future captain could not allow his men to laugh
at him.

At midday the two men had still not returned; so, in
his own room, Vel had a plate of barley soup, well
seasoned with aromatic herbs and fruit. Then he dressed
carefully, and was still not quite ready when the sound
of bronze-ringed wheels on the courtyard flagstones told
him his father was back. A few minutes later Aules came
into his room in high good humor, followed by Ibico.

"Well, are you ready? You don't look very gay. Last
night's wine was a bit strong for you, eh? Your mother
will have something to say when she hears I let you
drink."

"I'm fine, Father," said Vel, glancing sidelong at
Ibico. "Anyway, unless someone is going to tell her, I
don't see why Mother need ever know . . ."

"If you're thinking of Ibico, I've got some news you
won't like, my boy. But Velthur Tulumnes dug in his

heels and the price he offered me is more than generous. Anyway, Ibico's not coming on with us. He'll stay on in Populonia, in the house of Tulumnes."

Vel was astonished to find that he was in fact sorry to hear the news. After all, Ibico had been his tutor for years and, though he was sometimes as dreary as dullness itself, he would never forget the time they had spent together in Tarquinia and all he had learned from him.

"Have you sold him to Tulumnes? Oh Ibico, I'm sorry." The Greek raised his hand, indicating indifference, and smiled ironically as he spoke.

"I'm sorry to leave you too; but you're no longer a child, Vel, and when you go back to Tarquinia you won't need a tutor any longer. It is a teacher's fate to be abandoned by his pupils the moment they have learned to use the wings he has taught them to use. I have advised your father to send you to Athens when you are three years older to complete your education."

"Ibico will be very happy in the house of Tulumnes," said Aules. "Otherwise I wouldn't have sold him. He'll be in charge of the education of little Seia, our host's daughter, who's a nice child, they tell me. Velthur Tulumnes likes to follow Greek custom and keeps the women of his house shut up in their own apartments far from the sight of strangers, but he doesn't want them to remain ignorant, as so often happens with well-born Greek women. Seia has been taught music and dancing for years, and Ibico will teach her Greek and diction and all sorts of other marvels! All this will make her an excellent wife, and any good Tyrrhenian house will be glad to welcome her as its mistress."

As he said this he stared hard at Vel, who was arranging the folds of a light ceremonial cloak of beautiful blue material, woven by Uncle Larnth's weavers, and fringed with a border of ivy leaves.

"Tomorrow morning we'll finish loading," Aules went on. "All that's still to come is a little iron for the *Boar*. In the morning we'll choose the finished weapons; I want you to know exactly how much we're carrying, and I've made Ibico write it all down exactly—how much bronze, how much pig iron, and how much finished iron. Study it carefully, because the journey's long from here to Massalia, and the sea's always changeable. I'll give you a letter of introduction to Cele Aulenna who ordered the goods, as well."

"Are you afraid the journey's so dangerous, Father?" Vel asked softly.

Aules Pulena made no effort to reassure him.

"You've known for a long time that sea journeys are always dangerous, and this one particularly so, because we have to face the open sea. I've been as far as Massalia only once, with your grandfather, who was an able captain; and Ocno's done the journey three times, never without minor accidents. The goddess of fortune has always helped us, but we can't see into the future and the gods may change their minds. But tomorrow we'll sacrifice to Poseidon and the celestial gods whose mysterious name no one knows and who guide the thunderbolts of

Tinia. We'll make a rich offering, asking that Tulumnes' cargo may do well and be very valuable."

"That was a good idea of yours about the Greek vases, Father," said Vel.

Aules smiled.

"Vel, in our work it's always important to know people's weaknesses and what they have in their minds and in their hearts—that matters much more than how rich they are. But come along now. The city's on the move. It's not far to the theater, but there will be a great crowd."

Just then the curtain of buffalo hide across the door of Vel's room was raised, and Velthur Tulumnes, in the full glory of his ceremonial dress, stood in the doorway.

"If you're ready, my dear guests, we can set off. Though it isn't through my own merits, I can offer you one of the best places in the gallery, not far from Zilc and our triumphant hero. Your son's a fine, handsome lad, Aules," he added, for no apparent reason, and Vel looked at him, astounded. What did this unexpected compliment mean? And why was Father smiling and looking so pleased? It must be that they were pleased with the business they had done.

All three took their places in the large, luxurious, covered carriage, and Vel noticed with interest that another carriage, smaller than theirs, drawn by two white mules with a silver harness, was following them. This one, the ladies' carriage, was surmounted by closely drawn purple curtains, through which a pair of young eyes were watching the carriage ahead. The theater was not far. The Tulumnes' villa on the side of the hill had a long drive with cypresses on either side, which joined the winding road that came up from the harbor as far as the circular walls. Here was a door with an arch made of thick square-cut stones, decorated with stone sculptures representing the heads of men and dogs, and through it people of every age and kind were entering a paved square. Other carriages were trying to push in through the crowd and leather whips whistled through the air and cracked down warningly on the heads of the most obstinate. The roads of the high-built city were made like the spokes of a wheel and in the center of it, where they were now converging, was a large square in which local and foreign merchants displayed their wares and bartered. The tall columned facade of the temple, with steps leading up to it, stood on one side of the square—this was the citadel's highest point, and the columns and terra-cotta statues on the facade could be seen from the sea, welcoming returning sailors and newcomers to Populonia. A narrow passage led from the temple square to a smaller one, where a gay, noisy crowd was shoving its way into the open theater. This was a simple oval building, consisting of broad tiers of seats going down to the arena. Tulumnes and his guests got through with no trouble, for people stood aside respectfully to make way for Velthur's embroidered cloak, which was the sign of his priestly status. Vel kept peering around to see what had happened to the mule cart, and tripped over his father's sandals several times; at last Aules pushed him roughly and impatiently ahead. But when they were settled in the covered gallery on the comfortable cushions that covered the wooden benches, Vel caught the crowd's excitement.

"Sir, what's that strange thing in the arena?" He ventured to question Velthur Tulumnes, who still made him feel rather awestruck. Before his host could answer Aules spoke.

"You're still too young to have seen a Truia, but it's an old game with noble traditions, and we still have it in Tarquinia, though not very often."

"The horsemen have to ride through the maze and the one who gets out first is the winner," Velthur explained. Unless, of course, he's broken the fences or done anything else against the rules."

A very complicated, narrow path was made in the arena between fences made of posts and slats. The constant twists on the curve or at right angles were a hard test of skill for both men and horses, which had to be continually urged on or reined in to gain time.

"As your father says, it's an old game and reserved for the nobles. Only young men who belong to the oldest families can take part in it, and the horses need to be trained in a special way. They nearly all come from Vulci or from your Tarquinia, but the trainers are often Egyptian, or come from other countries that have been breaking horses for a very long time."

Vel was delighted to hear that Tarquinia trained the best horses and was just going to turn aside the compliment as good manners required him to, when a joyful shout from the crowd interrupted him. The seats were now all jammed with people, men, women, and children, and the women's round flat sun hats splashed bright colors among the bronzed faces of sailors and peasants. The wooden gallery, three stories high and supported on beams and posts, trembled all over; the spectators on the stories below leaped and shouted and stamped their feet on the floor, with a noise like distant thunder. Three young riders had come into the arena. They were mounted on small but slender and very agile horses, whose manes and tails were neatly plaited with ribbons or leather thongs and whose harness and bits gleamed with silver or copper ornaments. All the riders' efforts had been expended on their horses, for they themselves were quite naked, apart from a narrow strip of cloth around their hips and tightly laced sandals to protect their feet from the stirrups. Their long hair was

Wall painting;
5th Century B.C.

kept in place by gold diadems, and their splendid athletic bodies gleamed with the oil used to massage their
muscles. Two others followed the first three into the
arena and Velthur Tulumnes told his guests who they
were, describing the families they came from very precisely.

"Here in Populonia the nobles aren't what they used
to be. My father told me about the games in his day,
when the whole spectacle—the races, the expensive
training of the animals, the actors, and dancers, in fact
the entire business—was organized and paid for by the
nobles, for the glory of their own name and the enjoy-
ment of the people. Now the games are paid for out of
public funds and the horsemen are responsible only for
themselves and their horses. Still, there's plenty of bet-
ting and on a very large scale. Don't be surprised at the
end of the games, if you see people rolling off the seats
and wrapping their heads in their cloaks in despair at
losing a small fortune."

Vel realized that in spite of his criticisms, Velthur
would have been delighted if either he or a member of
his family had been allowed to take part in the games
reserved for the nobles. In Tarquinia the nobles also
lived in disdainful isolation, and he knew quite well that
there were games and meeting-places where neither he
nor any other Pulena would ever be admitted, however
rich they were, through their ships.

Aules Pulena smiled and shook his head.

"Times are changing faster now than they did when
our fathers were young, Velthur. It's the sea that gives

us Tyrrhenians wealth and prestige, not the land or the great estates of the nobles. Now that we've made good commercial treaties with the Carthaginians, the sea routes are open to our ships. Greece . . ."

A shrill trumpet blast interrupted him. At regular intervals along the entire curve of the seats, musicians, whose skill was famous in all the countries of the Great Sea, lifted their powerful curved trumpets and played a few rich, solemn notes. Zilc arrived, the highest civil official in Populonia at the time, and with him the triumphant hero whom Tulumnes had mentioned. Vel peered curiously at him, for he had never seen a man who had had the joy of being given a triumph. But the great man was rather disappointing, being anything but imposing—a gray fringe poked out from under the crown of oak leaves, delicately fashioned in pure gold, and his short weedy frame seemed lost in the triumphal tunic and the majestic folds of his painted cloak. He was holding an ivory scepter with a small gold eagle on the end of it, almost carelessly.

"Why, he's like a sailor! That's it, he's like Ocno. And he's so old! How could such a funny little man have deserved a triumph?"

He caught the end of what Velthur Tulumnes was saying to his father: ". . . an attack by Sardinian pirates. No, not directly in the gulf, they wouldn't have dared. But against the villagers south of the promontory. There's a man who really knows what he's doing! Those Sardinians are ferocious fighters, though here at Populonia there are some excellent Sardinian colonies, and I've had some first-rate workmen from among them. But many of them have been pirates, and we've still to fear the odd raid from them. But the last time they tried—four years ago, as I told you —they were given a good lesson. Tarchies Alethna destroyed their small ships while the pirates were ashore and captured a good many of them. Then he had them tortured and impaled on the beach and left them there for months, till the sea-winds and the weather finished them off, as an example to anyone else who might make another attempt. His son is called after him, young Tarchies, and he's in this race, second on the right on the black horse."

Vel shuddered with horror at the thought of those corpses on the beach, but thought it over and felt that the punishment was well deserved, even if hard. The pirates would have had no pity on the fishermen of those peaceful coastal villages. He looked with increased respect at the solemnly dressed little man taking up his position in the center of the gallery, whose son, looking bold and confident, was maneuvering his fine shining black horse in the arena.

The crowd's sudden silence told Vel the games were beginning. The judges, wearing dark gold-fringed cloaks and each carrying the curved baton used to arbitrate in the games, had already checked the riders and their mounts, and the restless horses were fidgeting about, pawing the ground. The priests of Turan, in whose honor the games were held, flung a handful of dark grains of incense into the great burner in front of the gallery. Scented smoke rose in the air, Zilc lowered his ivory baton, its eagle glittering in the sunshine, and the five horsemen were off. Each man must have made up his mind already which way he was to enter the maze, because no one hesitated a moment. Vel followed the progress of Tarchies, the triumphal hero's son, because he was the only one whose name he knew and because he had confidence in the quick, nervous horse whose quivering nostrils and lean, noble head showed its fine breeding. The Truia was not a violent race, but a game of skill, and the crowd roared and cheered. From the high gallery it was easy to follow the way the horsemen twisted about, but even those who knew most about the game could not predict the winner. Skill certainly counted, but luck came into it as well. The horses could only move slowly, and the whole art of their riding lay in the speed with which they managed to make their mounts shy and twist whenever they found the way ahead barred by a fence. It was all a matter of patience and muscles, and what really counted was not to get excited.

The first man who found a way out was not Tarchies Alethna, but an auburn-headed man as swift and agile as a ferret, riding a horse with white fetlocks that made it look as if it were wearing boots. He shot like an arrow out of the last straight section of the maze and the crowd yelled its applause. Tarchies Alethna was second, and less enthusiastically cheered. He moved off toward the dressing room with a gesture of anger spurring his horse, which reacted by nearly unseating him. The crowd roared with laughter and yelled a few remarks. The man who came third followed quickly, but a storm of laughter, yells, and protests awaited the last two unlucky horsemen who were stuck in the maze and seemed unable to find a way out. Sweating, desperate, maddened by the crowd's mockery, they spurred their foaming horses till they bled, and once they had lost their heads they made their mounts just as nervous as themselves.

At last one of the horses swerved, reared up on its hind legs almost vertically hurling its rider against the fence, and, to add to the man's ignominy, managed to find its own way out of the maze crazed with fear and anger, its stirrups dangling and bumping against its flanks. The crowd went wild. In the confusion it was hard to hear what anyone was saying. Meantime the other rider was doing no better. His horse had made up its mind to stay where it was; it stuck its head obstinately against the fence and, though the rider kept spurring it, it still wouldn't budge.

The audience was to lose patience, especially those on the lower seats whose view was obstructed by the high fence. Besides, after the Truia came boxing and wrestling, which the sailors, the peasants, and even the women were anxious to see. When the laughter changed to yells and screams and people began stamping their feet, Zilc pointed his ivory baton to the director of the games, whose high office entitled him to sit among the honored guests, and the trumpets signaled the end of the race. Aules Pulena, Tulumnes, and the others near them turned to each other to comment on the game, but Vel watched curiously as the slaves, with bronze axes and crowbars, rapidly dismantled, piled up, and removed the fence while the crowd hurled insults at the two riders.

"Just wait quietly, my lambs, they will soon be there to carry you out!"

"Look at the pair of them—like clumsy birds stuck in the nets!"

Other remarks were a good deal more vigorous. The circus audience was never generous, and here in Etruria where the games were becoming more of a show and less of a sporting event, those unlucky enough to annoy the public could expect no mercy.

Vel suddenly remembered the girl he had met in the garden, and turned to look up at the seats reserved for the nobles and civic authorities. It was not easy to spot Seia, but at last he saw her chatting with an imposing matron who was glittering with jewels. He wished he could catch her attention somehow, but in the crowded gallery it was hard to. So he kept staring at the two women in the hope that Seia would turn and look at him. But it was no use. She kept on chatting without glancing at the gallery where her father and his guests, including Vel, were sitting beside Zilc.

The arena was now cleared of the fences and a dozen slaves were raking the sand spread on the ground. Two pairs of athletes came into the arena, suddenly appearing from the dark dressing rooms where the contenders prepared for the show; they were completely naked, and their skin gleamed with oil. The first pair had leather straps wound tightly around their hands, wrists, and forearms up to the elbow, and on the knuckles the leather glittered with bronze, which meant that their blows could be murderous. The crowd cheered hard at first then fell suddenly silent, faces leaning forward, eyes gleaming, fingers gripping the edges of the seats and fidgeting with their clothes. An umpire walked forward solemnly, turned first to the gallery where the authorities sat, and greeted them with a nod, then held out his curved stick and touched the contenders, one by one, calling out their names loudly. After a prayer to Turan, goddess of the sea, he drew back and sat down not far from the boxers on a portable stool opened out for him by a small slave. The first two contenders stood in the middle of the arena, while the two others sat down to wait, leaning back against the enclosure fence. The crowd sighed faintly, as the two boxers began weaving around each other, never losing sight of each other, each watching carefully for the other's first move. Both were gigantic. One looked Etruscan, with thick black curls and large, black, melancholy, Tyrrhenian eyes. The other—Tulumnes told his guest quietly—was from Campania. His head was completely shaven and he had a brutal face with wide flattened nostrils and a low forehead. Suddenly, the Etruscan stopped studying his opponent and dropped all caution in a whirlwind attack that landed blows on his shoulder and temple; but the Campanian merely shook his head as if shaking off an insect, and retorted with some very violent blows that

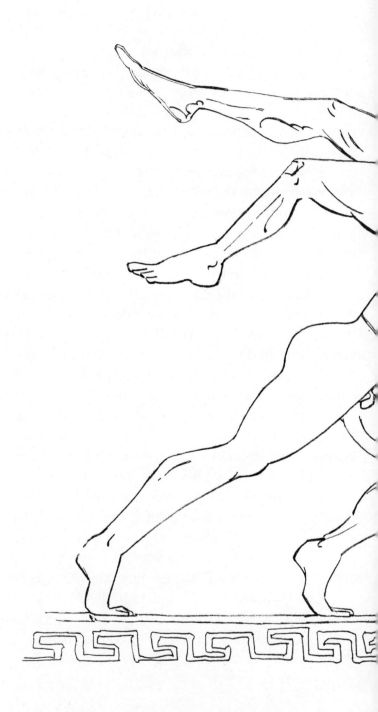

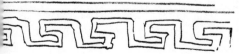

Wall painting;
5th Century B.C.

fell short, for the Etruscan, who was extremely agile and quick, avoided them by feinting. Vel realized the boxers were first-class and so did the crowd who were used to fights of this kind and could understand them. Suddenly, like an August storm, the fight broke loose—the boxers gave up playing defensively and hit out as hard as they could. The Etruscan had taken a few blows and seemed to have slowed down a little; every time a blow thudded home the crowd roared, then fell silent again. The show had gripped them so completely that the boxers' breathing, which grew progressively more painful, could be clearly heard. The Etruscan began to bleed at the mouth and his supporters shouted with dismay; Vel was backing him too, and turned to the gallery where Seia was sitting to see if the fact that his favorite was hurt had upset her. This time their eyes met and Vel was glad to see she was quite undisturbed by the brutal show.

"She's a real Tyrrhenian," he thought, "though her

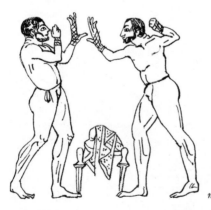

Circus scenes—detail of a mural painting; 5th Century B.C.

father would like to make a Greek of her. A bit of
blood doesn't worry her."

But this brief distraction made him miss the end of
the fight. The crowd had leaped up with a roar and
when Vel looked back to the arena he saw, to his surprise, that the Etruscan had a foot on the neck of his
fallen opponent whose blood was soaking into the sand.
The umpire went across to them solemnly, turned over
the Campanian's body with his baton, and looked carefully at his face. He was not dead, but he was certainly
beyond fighting for the time being. The crowd at fever
pitch talked over its bets, losers cursing the wretched
Campanian and winners sending kisses and cheers to the
Etruscan. As soon as two servants had dragged away
the wounded man's body and the winner had vanished
into the dressing room, the umpire repeated his cere-
mony of presentation for the next pair of fighters. But
they turned out to have nothing to do with fighting
as an art. It was not a case of avoiding blows; success
was all a matter of brute force. This kind of show meant
nothing to Vel, but the sailors and dockers liked it and
urged the two men on enthusiastically. There were no
intervals in the fight and one or the other of the men
would probably lose his life, because it was thought very
dishonorable to give in. But this time the weaker of the
two was lucky enough to be knocked out by a terrible
blow from his opponent; he lay in the arena, and the
fact that he had fainted saved his life. Velthur Tulumnes
shrugged with annoyance.

"The people won't be too pleased. Now, barring accidents, nobody will be killed, and the audience will be disappointed. Next there's pole vaulting and high jumping, climbing the greasy pole and other fairly dull little games."

"Won't you have chariot races?" asked Vel, disappointed not to see his favorite sport.

"Not at feasts in honor of Turan. We have foot racing, throwing the discus—there are some real champions at that here—and the great dance in mime. It's not as important as the one at the feasts of Fufluns whom your Ibico must call Dionysus, son of Zeus and Semele. Fufluns is the tutelary god of our city, which takes its name from him. The dances celebrated in his honor are marvelous, and the dancers are inspired by wine—Fufluns gave it to man, you know, by showing him how to cultivate the vine. But the dances in honor of the great goddess of the sea Turan-Aphrodite are beautiful as well, and our women like them in particular, because Turan is the goddess of love."

In the arena the games continued as planned, but the audience no longer cared much. The men were still discussing the boxing and the fight, or were playing dice while the women were chattering. Dice was a very popular and a very old Etruscan game, and though ordinary people could not hazard large sums or valuable property like the nobles and the rich, they still played excitedly wherever they happened to be and whatever the stakes —even if it was only a goblet of wine. It was the greasy pole climbing contest that regained the audience's attention. Youngsters who tried to climb it kept sliding back

Aphrodite (Turan); *500 B.C.*

clumsily, and the crowd laughed and jeered; at last two sailors, whose constant exercise on the masts and rigging stood them in good stead, managed to get to the top and took down some of the prizes hung there—poultry, salted legs of pork and veal, and clothing.

But everyone was glad when the trumpets announced the end of the games and the auburn-haired horseman, the Etruscan boxer, and the winning fighter came up to Zilc to get their prizes. The winner of the Truia got a simple laurel crown, for the games reserved for the aristocracy were not played for valuable prizes; but the others, being professionals, got very expensive prizes as well as their Greek-style crown. The crowd applauded warmly and shouted the athletes' names. For several days these would be bandied about in taverns and hovels as respectfully as the names of the gods. The prize-giving over, the servants ran onto the arena to clear it and to rake over the sand.

The crowd was quieter now, as if exhausted by the brutal show. Twilight was falling, the cloudless sky had turned fiery red, and the arena was gradually touched by purple shadows. Several young men, circus servants, came over and raised the canopy that hung from the wooden roof of the gallery. The women covered their heads and shoulders with colored veils. Vel glanced at where Seia was sitting and saw a woman slave laying a rich rug of light woolen material on the two womens' laps. Seia looked back at him, then quickly looked away.

The musicians were coming into the arena. First came

the trumpeters, carrying smaller instruments than those
which had signaled the races. They were bronze and of
all kinds of shapes. Etruscan craftsmen had invented
them and were famous for it throughout the world.
Then came the aulos-players with their double or plain
flutes, and lastly the lyre players with their beautiful
seven-stringed instruments made of silver and valuable
woods sometimes inlaid with ivory. The fashion for
these had come from Greece. All the musicians were
young and beautifully dressed, their hair carefully arranged and plaited with ribbons and jewels, and they
wore diadems of silver and gold, necklaces, and bracelets. Professional musicians, in Populonia as in the rest
of Etruria, enjoyed special prestige and earned a great
deal. But Vel thought them all rather effeminate and
disliked their airs and graces and their carefully curled
hair.

The excitement increased when the dancers came in.
They were all young, apart from the leading dancer
who was an oldish priest of Turan, since the dances
were in his honor. After the usual prayer to him, the
musicians started playing a slow, monotonous song, first
on the flutes, then accompanied by the stringed instruments. The dancers moved in time to the music, slowly
and gracefully, their hands, wrists, and bare arms unfolding in a flower-like way, while their bodies were
nearly still. The leading priest was, despite his age, the
best of all. The music, which had a very small range of
notes, had the dreamy rhythm of an oriental lullaby—
something Egyptian or Persian perhaps—but suddenly

Wall painting; 5th Century B.C.

the trumpets joined in as well as two small drums held by the players between their knees and struck with fingers as stiff as small hammers.

The dancing at once grew faster: legs were now moving swiftly, feet thudding on the sand in a shorter rhythm. Pleated garments began unfolding, and flapping like sails blown madly by the wind; the music began hammering and the dancers' bodies flowed backwards and forwards, arms upflung, feet invisible except as the swirl of golden sandals. The crowd became more and more affected by the music. Faces mirrored the excitement and grew almost as heated as those of the dancers. Mouths hung open, while the setting sun reddened clothes and bodies, sand and instruments, and gave the whole picture a savage splendor. Finally on a shrill, loud trumpet-note from the exhausted musicians, the dance ended, and the dancers stilled like birds wounded in flight, then fell on the sand, their limbs limp and uncontrolled. For a second Vel felt physical pain, as if something—like a tight string—had snapped in his head.

VI.

OMENS AND PREDICTIONS

Vel slept deeply the night after the circus show and the rich banquet that followed in Tulumnes' honor. But early in the morning the night gives way to a time of milky pallor, and there comes a vague, mysterious, shifting time accompanied by dreams—and whether these are images put out by the sleeper who has something on his mind or real omens that come as messages from the unknown world of spirits, kind or inimical, no one can tell. Vel thought he saw the *Captain* in full sail, riding fast over a sea that was dark and yet transparent. On her deck was a figure like his father, but when he looked at its face he realized he could see nothing— just a white spot, eyeless, featureless. And when he was about to call a greeting at the passing ship, he saw something moving very slowly and gracefully on top of the

Winged female demon ("Lasa") –
from a duck-shaped pitcher of terra-cotta;
4th Century B.C.

main mast and recognized the dancer from the temple
of Turan. It couldn't be anyone else, with those loose
saffron robes that seemed to form wings as they moved
—in fact they *were* wings! And it wasn't the dancer
from the temple of Turan, but a great Lasa, the winged
guardian spirit that protects man and serves him. But
soon Vel couldn't see the guardian spirit either, because
it started whirling dizzily around, faster and faster, and
from its wings came a cold wind of death, that dragged
ship and sailors, and the spectral faceless captain still
standing on the bridge, down to perdition in a whirlpool.

Vel leaped out of bed, screaming and sweating, and
saw the worried face of his father who was holding him
by the shoulders and still trying to shake him off. Vel
sheltered in his arms as he had done when he woke from
a nightmare as a child—after eating unripe fruit or too
many pigs' trotters or being chased by the porter's big
dog.

"The waterspout!" he babbled. I saw the waterspout.
But it was the Lasa that called it up, I'm certain—the

Lasa with its huge yellow wings. And you had no eyes or face or anything."

Aules Pulena smiled and winked at his son.

"Ah, Vel! This is what happens when you drink the terrible wines of Cyprus and Corinth instead of the good little wines from our own hills. This is just one reason why I disapprove of Velthur Tulumnes' passion for things Greek—Greek wine doesn't suit Etruscan stomachs. And let's hope Ocno's managed to keep his boys away from the taverns in the harbor. Don't worry, son! On board you'll find others who can't carry resinous wine any better than you can. As for the Lasa,"—and here Aules bowed reverently, as he did when he mentioned any divine being—"Before leaving we'll sacrifice to the gods of the Twelve Celestial Houses. Yesterday I sent a sheep and a lamb to the priest of Poseidon, and the same offering to the most famous soothsayer in Populonia. He'll have studied its liver for us, and he'll tell us if the journey is propitious. But now listen."

Aules Pulena's face became very serious and Vel, forgetting his nightmare, glanced curiously at a large roll of waxed cloth his father was taking from the folds of his tunic.

"I've got one just the same. It's a list of the goods on the *Boar*. I've also got the list of what we've got on the *Captain*, of course, but this is the only one you need. There's bronze and iron to the value of two Greek talents—a fortune! I've arranged the whole business with Cele Aulenna, as I told you. If you get to Massalia before me . . ."

Vel shuddered, but his father seized his arm and staring imperiously into his face continued,

"I said *before* me, not *without* me! Now, if you and Ocno are cleverer or luckier than I, you'll go to Cele Aulenna and get him to give you two talents' worth of goods. I've made a list here of the goods you must take on at Massalia; leather, first of all, skins that savage tribes from the interior bring to the coast; and then silver in the form of Greek coins, and another valuable material you may not have seen, called amber. Don't worry, Cele Aulenna won't cheat you when you show him this letter and my ring with the seal of the leopards." As he said this, Aules took a large gold ring off his little finger, and gave it to Vel, together with a small roll of Egyptian papyrus. Vel knew papyrus was much prized for writing on and was used for messages and letters that were not too long. The ring was identical with the one his father wore on his middle finger, only smaller; both were made of pure yellow gold, with a long narrow oval in the middle that had two leopards cut into it, their tails held high and turned up over the backs, their proud mouths gaping. Laid on hot wax, it would leave their image in relief, and it was the seal of the Pulenas known for decades along the shores of the Great Sea.

Vel took it, and proudly put it on the middle finger of his right hand, which it fit almost perfectly. He was so intent on looking at it that he hardly heard what his father was saying, until a few words suddenly struck him.

". . . and since you're a man, it is now time to think of finding you a wife!"

"But father!" protested Vel, scarlet in the face. "I'm not going to get married, really I'm not!"

At the sight of his frightened face Aules burst out laughing.

"Nor do I mean you to have a wife right away, you silly! For the moment, I just wanted to choose a bride for you, to betroth you. But if you really can't bear the idea . . ."

"No, no, women are all frightful!" Vel answered stubbornly. "You can't talk to them seriously and you never know when they're going to start teasing you. They always do it suddenly."

Aules nodded understandingly.

"You're right, my boy. But you see, the Pulenas are always betrothed soon after they've reached their twelfth year and they've always married women from merchant families—it's our tradition. And as Velthur Tulumnes didn't seem to dislike the idea of giving you his daughter . . ."

"Seia?" Vel burst out and realized at once that he had given himself away like a fool. His father looked at him with such astonishment that it was hard to believe it was faked.

"So you know the daughter of Velthur Tulumnes? But how is that possible? Aha, so that's why you didn't want to get involved! I suppose you found her ugly, vulgar, ignorant!"

"No, no, she's pretty and she seems very well brought

up," Vel hastily admitted. "But . . . I'm afraid she doesn't like me, and that's a fact! Yesterday evening she didn't even look at me at the circus, and she had told me herself where she would be sitting!"

"Ah, so that's why you were wriggling about on your seat as if you'd been nipped by a spider," said Aules Pulena. His voice was serious, but his eyes were laughing. "If that's all that's worrying you, stop. Do you remember what I said to Velthur Tulumnes about something being added to the price of my Greek vases? Seia is promised to you, and when we return to Tarquinia we'll take her to your mother, to make her into a good wife for you, the last of the Pulenas to bear our ancient name."

Vel was pleased, but slightly disconcerted, too, by the speed of events. First his twelfth year, then the journey, now a wife! But he soon got used to the idea. Besides, it would not have been much use opposing it—that much he realized. Traditionally, his father had every right to decide for him. He liked Seia, and in any case, before he got married—which still seemed an extraordinarily funny notion—there was the journey to Massalia and the Pulena seal shining splendidly on his finger.

He jumped out of bed.

"Oh Father, let's go, let's get off. I feel I've been sleeping and sleeping, as if Hypnos, the god of sleep, had enchanted me. I'm longing to see the *Blue Boar* and Ocno and Vipis! I'll put these notes and figures in my box and I really won't lose them. We've still got weapons and metal things to choose; there's no time to lose, Father!"

Aules laughed.

"If Hypnos, the god of sleep, was rocking you before, it's Hermes, the god of trade, who's urging you on now. Let's get down to the harbor, because there are the final things to see to."

Vel and his father did not see their host, who was still in his room, but, as everything was now settled, Aules decided to wait for him down at the harbor and the light carriage quickly took him there. While they were still on the quayside, beside which the *Boar* lay calmly at anchor with the dew on her planks, Vel heard Ocno's familiar voice roaring out curses at his men, calling on all the gods of sea and sky and wondering why they failed to hurl thunderbolts at those good-for-nothing numbskulls—brainless nincompoops—the most hopeless bunch of idiots it had ever been his misfortune to see on a ship.

Aules stopped under the keel, cupped his hands around his mouth, and shouted.

"Hey, old fellow, let them get on with it and come and receive your master!"

Ocno's dishevelled gray head poked up over the ship's side, his everlasting cap pulled down to his eyebrows.

"May the dawn favor you and your son, Sir! Your servant's glad to see you. As for you, you wretched miserable remains of a misspent life, you ruinous old carcass you . . ." he went on, turning to an unlucky fellow untangling a rope to tie to a bucket, and looking as timid and dejected as a dog scared of a kick.

"Drop it, Ocno. I want to know where Tulumnes' steward is."

"Sir, in these two days I've seen more Greeks than I ever want to see the rest of my life. It's incredible the way these locusts come swarming around our shores. Wherever you set foot they've set up colonies. But the particular one you're looking for I don't happen to have seen this morning. I've nearly finished loading up the *Boar*, though."

But Vel's sharp eyes had already seen the plump Greek hurrying across to them, smiling.

"Father, the steward's just coming," he said.

"Talk of the devil," said the irrepressible Ocno, vanishing at once behind the ship's side, as if someone had pulled him back by the legs.

The sheets and ingots of iron and bronze obtained in the foundry were finished in the workshop next door. There, too, was the constant clang of blows on anvils, but these, though numerous, were smaller than the enormous one Vel had seen two days earlier. In a small warehouse were stored the finished weapons—old-fashioned helmets with pointed bronze crests and rigid cheek coverings, or else bronze marions that held waving feathers; and Greek-style helmets with movable coverings for the cheeks and holders for long horsehair plumes. The old-fashioned helmets were Etruscan, and so were the few doubleheaded battle axes, which were now very rarely made. People preferred short, pointed swords and light javelins, or else another type of sword

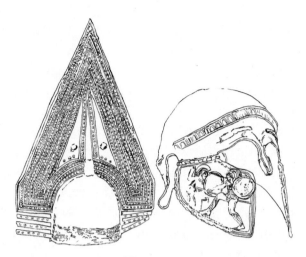

A) *Large bronze helmet; 7th Century B.C.*
B) *Helmet; undated.*

—thin and curved; since cavalry had taken over entirely from chariots in battle, weapons that were more easily handled were needed. There were also tidy stacks of shields, either long or round, and suits of armor that looked like bodies beheaded by some evil spell. A soldier could have equipped himself there completely for any battle, either for the infantry or for the cavalry. While Aules chose his cargo, followed by the steward with his inseparable abacus, Vel walked behind them, his ears cocked for the dry click of the wooden beads, his eyes peering greedily around at all these marvels. One of the smiths came after them, a one-eyed giant who was the workshop foreman—and Vel remembered with a shudder the accident he had seen the day he arrived. This man would pick up a shield, helmet, or breastplate and without speaking demonstrate its solidity or lightness by weighing it in his hand or trying to bend it—a thing he could never manage, even with his enormous muscular arms that gleamed with sweat.

Aules Pulena chose two piles of weapons, the best in every way, for looks as well as quality, were to go on the *Captain* and were for the Greek colonists at Massalia. The others—axes, knives, heavy shields, and stouter helmets without feathers or ornaments—would be sold by Cele Aulenna to the half-savage tribes of the interior who came into Massalia to exchange their skins for metal goods they could not make themselves. These would be the *Boar*'s cargo.

When they had all been chosen, the day was almost half over and Vel was beginning to feel tired. Once outside the dark workshop, he drew a deep breath to get the sooty air out of his lungs and gazed lovingly at his beloved *Boar,* where he had spent such happy days on the clean, salt-smelling sea. From the way his father squared his shoulders, Vel realized he felt just the same sense of relief, and the pair of them smiled at each other.

Below the *Boar*'s main deck they found Velthur Tulumnes talking to the grumpy Ocno—who had not even bothered to come down and was talking over the ship's side. Tactfully Velthur had refrained from joining them in the workshop, to avoid giving them the impression that he was keeping an eye on their choice of goods. In any case, he trusted his Greek steward completely. Now he never even mentioned the weapons but asked politely how they were, and Vel, now that he knew about their future relationship, watched him much more curiously than before. But he knew that the two men would never speak of him and Seia while he was there; to talk officially to a boy about his plans would lower the head of the family's prestige. Vel was sure Seia knew she had been promised to him, and would have loved to know how she had taken it. But the talk was now all about their departure. Velthur Tulumnes approved of the way Aules had made offerings at the temple and to the soothsayer, and said they must visit the old man right away to see what he had to tell them. Ocno, with the familiarity of a man who was almost one of the family and could say what he wanted, gave his views on the matter.

"At Cere we sprinkled wine and milk on the bow before sailing, so that the ship's spirit would set off on the journey refreshed. And the Phoenicians, who really know the sea, pour the blood of an animal that's had its throat cut onto it. The master can talk to the soothsayer all he likes, but I'm going to sacrifice a kid before dawn tomorrow and give the bow some wine and milk for good measure."

"A kid?" said Aules, astonished. "By all the sea-monsters, Ocno, what for? I've never seen you offer more than a goose or a pair of doves."

"Quite true, sir," said Ocno, lowering his voice, while his face became gloomy. "But this isn't a trip like the others. Crossing the sea to the island of Corsica isn't hard, but after that we've got to leave the island and cross the Great Gulf and follow those rocky coasts full of currents. And what about Massalia? What sort of welcome do you think we'll get there from the Greek colonists?"

"You know perfectly well they allow trade with us, in fact they encourage it. What else can they do? They need metal and cloth and leather and weapons. Massalia's a city of merchants, not of industrialists, and it lives by the sea. War's one thing, trading's another. And then, such a distant war, after all! Of course, fifty years ago, after Alalia, we couldn't have landed near the Greek colonists, but it's a long time since then and time is a goddess with a very short memory. Besides, Cele Aulenna's Etruscan and he's lived in Massalia for fifteen years. So finish your loading, because we'll weigh anchor at dawn tomorrow. And you can curse and swear all you like at those men of ours, because I want them on their toes tomorrow!"

Ocno pressed his lips stubbornly together but said nothing; merely stared after the three as they walked away. But, without being seen or even turning, Vel managed to show him his wonderful ring by swinging his hand up behind his back and waving it about.

The soothsayer lived high up in the city, and out of politeness and in order to serve as intermediary, Velthur Tulumnes took his guests there. Because of his own priestly office, he considered the soothsayer a kind of colleague.

It was not snobbishness that made the soothsayer choose to live in this elegant district, but because for years he had been studying the flight of birds, which was extremely important in foreseeing the future. His house was not only perched high on the hillside, but had a strange kind of tower next door to it with a small wooden staircase in it leading up to some very narrow windows. From this he could study the flight of birds and see out over an enormous distance. For some reason Vel had expected to find a decrepit old man with white hair, a beard like the Greek philosophers, and flowing robes. Instead, a small, scraggy man, yellow-faced as a result of malaria caught in some swampy district on the Tyrrhenian coast, came up and welcomed them inform-ally, and Vel was not particularly impressed. Only his small piercing black eyes glittered with an almost re-pulsive expression in his papyrus-colored face. The girl who was with him seemed very much nicer, and although she was clearly not a slave, her clothes were very simple. Her expression was extremely gentle and she seemed fond of the unattractive creature, hurrying about look-ing after him and his visitors, bringing seats and stools and goblets and finally a clay jar of wine, which the moment its seal was broken, sent a strong scent of aromatic herbs into the small room where they were sitting. Before Tulumnes, in his precise, florid way, had finished asking for the information his guests were seeking, the soothsayer put up a hand to ask for silence.

"I examined the livers of the sheep and the lamb which were sent to me. Though I've been so busy these last few days that I was afraid I'd be choked with work. There were the feasts of Turan and people flooding into town wanting to discover the wishes of the gods, which is just as it should be, for in order to take the right road and avoid mistakes a man must know the divine dispositions. I wonder what the use is of living for the moment, as the Greeks do, and making the gods into superior but quite ordinary beings, who quarrel among themselves as they do in the legends of Homer and turn their blind rage or their equally blind benevolence onto man? The divine is among us, but it doesn't have the same face as our human passions, and mortal eyes cannot understand the sacred signs without the mediation of the priest and of those who can divine the will of the gods."

"And you, noble Tlesmas, are one of the best seers we have," Tulumnes interrupted, though very respectfully. "You were saying, now—about the sheep's liver?"

"I looked at the liver with my bronze tablet on which the gods' names are written, and also those whose sacred names must not be pronounced by the uninitiated."

Vel disliked soothsayers who always made him feel scared and uneasy. Ibico, who was frankly skeptical about them, had told him about all kinds of things that looked miraculous performed by those he scornfully called "wizards" which had quite clearly and logically been impossible without trickery. He had told him there were "wizards" of the same sort in Greece, especially in a half-barbarous district called Thessaly, and Vel, though half inclined to take a realistic view of things, was reluctant to give up his Etruscan feeling that life was constantly intermingled with the divine. This might mean the heavenly spirits or it might mean the spirits of his forebears, whom Vel was sure had not vanished entirely in the dust of their colored tombs; or it might be the presiding spirit of the world, the soul of things which was equally alive in him, and in his ship, and in the waves of the sea, and in the clouds of the sky. Now, as the small yellow man talked and talked, using solemn, difficult words, Vel, slightly bewildered by the strong smell of the wine, could hardly follow what he was saying. The girl, who was sitting on a leather cushion by the window, occasionally glanced furtively at the visitors and seemed more interested in them than in the old man's words. But Aules Pulena was listening attentively, and so was Velthur, who looked as pleased as a man who has promised a good show and finds it lives up to his expectations. Vel was waiting impatiently for the time to leave and disrespectfully watching the way the soothsayer's mouth moved—he seemed to be suffering from a nervous tic, and every three words or so his lips twisted and his right nostril, eyelid, and eyelash moved.

Then suddenly something changed. Until now the prophet had been saying that the sheep's liver promised the Pulenas a fairly fortunate voyage, but now, as he stared hard at a kind of complicated drawing full of names and incomprehensible signs, he peeped furtively at Aules Pulena's face, while his own slowly darkened.

"Like the shadow of a cloud over the deck of a ship that gradually devours it from stem to stern," thought Vel, uneasy without knowing why. The soothsayer stopped, then patiently started running his fingertip over the squiggles again. Once again he stopped, and looked thoughtfully at Aules.

"Well, soothsayer, what have you read in the divine

will?" Aules Pulena asked, firmly but seriously. "It's something that concerns me, isn't it?"

The little man seemed oddly annoyed.

"I'm not a fortune teller, as so many claim to be, and I can't tell exactly what the gods have in store for you. It is just that I have found a sign I don't like."

"But that's just what I want to know. So speak up, old man. Will my journey not be successful?"

"Your *journey* will end successfully, as I have told you already, noble Pulena, but I see nothing there that speaks of *your* happy return."

At these words the room seemed to turn cold, but Aules lost none of his calm.

"You didn't see this in the sheep's liver, though, did you? You were looking at my face just now, and it was there you read something that worried you."

"You're sharp-witted, merchant. But no one is sharp-witted enough to escape his ordained end—you know that yourself, for you realized I saw that your end is fairly near."

Tulumnes interposed nervously, trying to disperse the sudden uneasiness.

"Oh come, come! The gods are looking favorably on your trip—the sheep's entrails said so! Well then! All of us have to end sometime, and none of us can escape it. But wise as you are, and skilled in the art of divination, can you tell when that end will come—on what day, at what hour? No, of course not. So your calculations and your prophecies may be mistaken. Only on this subject,

Detail of a sculpture; 5th-4th Century B.C.

of course," he added hastily, fearful of offending the little man who now frightened him.

The old man smiled.

"I should be very stupid to contradict you. I have said only what I thought I saw, but my eyes are not omniscient."

"We thank you for what you have told us," said Aules Pulena. "You have been honest, and I don't want to consider whether what you have said is true or not. When you set off on a journey you don't want to take gloomy thoughts with you—they're a worse threat to a ship than a storm is. We must trust in the goodness of Poseidon and the winds that rule the waves . . ."

"And in the stoutness of the ship!" Vel broke in, not understanding why the others burst out laughing. Surely he hadn't said anything silly! But their laughter made them feel at ease again; it was like a sea breeze blowing away clouds.

"The younger generation!" said Aules Pulena, with pride and melancholy in his voice together.

But Vel was worried by what the soothsayer had said and his uneasiness remained when they returned to the house; in fact he could not enjoy the plain meal of cheese and fruit they were served. Tulumnes noticed.

"Your son has no appetite, Aules," he said. "Or do you think he's trying to keep an empty head and stomach for the banquet this evening? If he's so wise, though still so young, he knows women don't like to see what Dionysus does to men. Someone must have told him there's a great farewell feast in the house of Tulumnes, and that on this occasion the ladies of the house will leave their private apartments."

And he burst out laughing when he saw Vel turn crimson at this direct reference to Seia.

In any case, he was not at all sure he wanted to see her; in fact, he was scared of her sharp tongue and was sure that she would be much the more unruffled of the two of them. But he wanted to look his best, and dressed very carefully after a bath in a large wooden basin which two slaves had filled with warm water. Things were not as he had imagined them, though. The lady of the house, who had simple manners and a placid expression, was not the least bit alarming.

"Mother's much more beautiful," he said to himself, with pride. She had the place of honor between her husband and Aules Pulena, on the same couch as they were, and the two children sat far apart with a whole row of Tulumnes cousins and relations between them, peeping furtively and almost scowlingly at each other.

Seia was very richly dressed and looked like a doll glittering with jewels; she sat rather stiffly with her feet dangling off the sofa, looking pleased with herself and absorbed in her new dignity. Vel could scarcely believe it was the same child who had challenged him in the garden, and then in the theater. So his memory of the banquet was a disagreeable one—he remembered how people had stared, the men more kindly, the women more openly curious, smiling and making remarks behind their ringed fingers or their fans. Luckily it was not a real betrothal party—this was to be held when they

Antefix; 6th-5th Century B.C.

came back and stopped at Populonia for the second time with all the ceremonies and rites involved in exchanging a solemn promise. So the women were able to retire quite early with a great rustling of dresses taking with them the little girl whom they kept in their midst, like a flower surrounded by a swarm of large bright butterflies.

At last the men could talk freely without having to consider the ladies, and this time Vel stoutly resisted the sleepiness that threatened him, though the scent of flowers, the soft flute music, and the slow, graceful movements of the dancers engaged by Velthur Tulumnes for the banquet, all made it difficult to do so. He managed to stay awake and listened delightedly when his father recalled voyages to the East in the opposite direction from those the Greeks had made centuries earlier from Ionia to the West along the coast of Africa, then along the Iberian shores to the mouth of the Rhone River, whose yellow waters poured into the Ligurian Sea, not far from Massalia; or else across the straits that Homer had sung of, when the monsters Scylle and Charibdys stood on either side, greedily waiting for any bold ship that attempted to make the crossing. And others spoke too, for there were seafarers at Populonia; indeed the whole place seemed born from the sea, like Turan-Aphrodite, with its rows of houses on the beach and even the old ancestral tombs almost within reach of the waves. Vel felt closer to these bold spirits—half merchants, half explorers—than to his future father-in-law, who sat listening to them with his polite host's smile, but was clearly more interested in what they had to say about valuable cargoes that filled the ships' holds with exotic scents.

That evening seemed to confirm Vel's maturity. He no longer looked with childish glee at the Pulenas' ring glowing on his finger, but with family pride: he must continue to bring it honor on the seas.

VII.

SAILS ON THE HIGH SEAS

Next morning the Pulenas took leave of their host—
who was now a relation—ceremoniously but fast. The
sun had not yet risen and a light but constant breeze
was blowing from inland: ideal weather for setting sail.
Behind the rocks of Populonia dawn was beginning to
lighten the sky.

Vel had already packed his box carefully and tidily.
Ocno always said that a careless, untidy sailor was a
sailor with little to lose. It was odd, when he was on
land, Vel felt bound to the house he was living in and
to the authority of whoever was teaching him. Till now,
this had been Ibico. But at the start of his voyage, the
smell of the sea and the figure of Ocno grew more and
more important in his mind, and the rest vanished hazily
into the distance.

In the carriage he discussed with his father—or rather Aules spoke, and Vel listened—the route they were to follow. The ox skin that had hung on the wall in Tarquinia had reappeared. Vel had to learn by heart the blue and clay-red signs which one of Aules Pulena's clerks, a talented painter, had drawn on it. But this was easy enough. There was the dark shore of the Tyrrhenian lands with red marks indicating Cere, Tarquinia, and Populonia. There was the irregular outline of the island of Etalia where the mines were. And lower down, further south, small uninhabited islands were drawn in very precisely. Then came the first stretch of blue sea as far as a curious promontory shaped like a nose—the island of Corsica: this was the first place they were bound to stop at, as Vel already knew. Because the ships were loaded with cargo and somewhat slower than usual, it would not be possible to take enough water to last out the rest of the voyage.

"Here, we pick up water; there's a woody bay I know where we'll find it, and only shepherds live there, gentle souls who won't bother us," said Aules, following the red line with his finger that touched at Corsica. "Perhaps they won't even appear, because they're afraid of pirate raids, though for a long time they've been extremely rare and the work of some lone wolf, not a band of them. But it's still possible to get a fishing boat and a crew of desperadoes—thieves or deserters who've managed to escape the law, ours or that of Greece or Phoenicia."

"Are there really pirate raids still?" asked Vel.

"Yes, they can still happen. Especially to capture slaves to sell in Eastern markets. But the shepherds don't have their villages near the shore—they build their huts a bit inland, and down by the sea they just have towers made of huge piled-up stones where they keep a man on watch who sees anyone landing and soon gives the alarm if he realizes they're up to no good. But they'll let us have water, and that's all that matters." His fingertip kept slowly curving westward around the Ligurian gulf, several miles out from the shore.

"Why don't we cut straight across the gulf of Massalia from the island?" asked Vel. "It would save a lot of time." Then he realized he was talking nonsense and turned scarlet. "What a fool I am—I suppose we can't because of the currents."

"That's right. Think before you speak, not afterwards. We follow the curve of the gulf because of the currents—it's not quite the way it's drawn here. But Ocno will tell you all about it during the voyage. He's seen this map himself, but he really has no need for it. At sea he follows invisible routes, guided by the stars and the winds, but sometimes I suspect he's just following his nose. He knows the sea better than a dolphin!"

Vel laughed at the idea of the old helmsman sniffing the route out from the bow like a dog following the scent of a deer, and he was still laughing when he got down from the carriage. On the *Captain*'s main mast the largest sail was already hoisted, and all the rest above it were already unfurled. The *Boar* also had only a single small sail hoisted, but both ships found them quite enough to catch the wind as soon as the great anchors were raised; the moorings had already been cut and the anchors were tugging desperately at their hawsers.

Aules laid his hand on Vel's shoulder, looked straight at him, and shook him fondly.

"We'll be waiting for you in Corsica, where the bay opens out. Mind you, don't get lost in that old turtle of yours."

"Sea turtles are fast swimmers," Vel wanted to retort, but not daring to he just winked at his father. Aules smiled faintly and turned away, and walked firmly across to the *Captain* with one of Velthur's servants behind him carrying his box. Vel hitched his own up onto his shoulder and climbed happily up the narrow gangplank.

"Hey!" He flung his box down on the deck and bounded astern where Ocno was at the rudder.

"Poseidon guard you, Ocno! I'm so glad to see you! I have so much to tell you it will take the whole morning!"

The old man looked at him in a way he looked at no one else—half ironical, half affectionate—and said with studied indifference, "Now, let's see if I can guess. Am I right or do my old eyes detect that there's more gold glittering on your right hand than there was when you took off from our humble *Boar* to enjoy yourself with Velthur Tulumnes? That's the Pulena leopards you've got there, sir."

"What's all this *sir* about, you old wolf?" said Vel, punching Ocno's muscular arm. "The Pulena leopards certainly won't spare me the weight of those great hands of yours when you're in a rage—as you are at least once a day may the gods protect me!"

"Quite right, sir, quite right! And if you were the Great King's minister or the Pharaoh of Egypt's prospective son-in-law, you'd still be my own lad on the *Blue Boar!*"

"Son-in-law! Why, you prize devil, whoever told you about my betrothal? How is it you get to know everything? Were those wretched ears of yours long enough to get right up the hill and into the house of Tulumnes?"

"I was just using that as an example, sir—don't get worked up! But if I had wanted to hear of it, all I would have had to do was to go to the market yesterday morning, where they bring in fruits and vegetables from the country and fish still alive from the sea, and hover near a crowd of old women and idlers hanging around a couple of gossipy slaves and a kitchen boy, and listen to what they were saying about the excitement up at Tulumnes'. Why, if I had done that I would soon have known there was something up. The finest fish and crabs and mussels they wanted, the choicest country vegetables and curds and milk and the gods only know what else!"

"Oh, you know all about it," muttered Vel, reddening. "And what did Tulumnes' servants say?"

"That poor Seia, Velthur Tulumnes' daughter, was promised to some mysterious stranger from afar. That none of them—slaves or kitchen boys—had seen him close up, but the gardeners and the banquet hall servants said he has twisted legs and hairy ears, a wall eye and a couple of sharp horns on his head, only they couldn't be sure of that under the banquet wreath!"

Ocno burst out laughing, as Vel opened his eyes wide and prepared to lose his temper. But the old man was obviously enjoying it so much that Vel decided not to give him the satisfaction of watching him explode and to ignore his witticisms in a dignified way.

"Well, who cares about market gossip? Slaves will be slaves. Now we're off, praise heaven. Have you made the sacrifices you told us about?"

"If you look over the bow and try not to fall into the sea you'll find the *Boar*'s head dripping with milk and wine and the blood of a pretty little kid. It wasn't just to collect the gossip that I went to the market, sir. And Vipis, who's got some blood in his veins that isn't exactly Tyrrhenian, you know, and has a real live witch from the mountains of Campania somewhere in his background . . . But your tutor will say I'm filling your head with old wives' tales! Where is he, by the way, where's he gone and hidden himself? Is he still polishing his shoes and thinking I'd hang around for hours, waiting for him when the *Captain*'s already weighed anchor?"

"Aha, so you don't really know everything, you old rascal," cried Vel, delighted with himself. "You didn't know that now, did you? Well, prepare for a fine surprise!"

"The Greek got drunk, slipped on the stairs and broke his neck?"

"No, you old wretch. Father's sold him to Velthur Tulumnes, as tutor to my betrothed . . . well, to his daughter Seia, that is. Father said I didn't need him anymore and that you can teach me all I need to know much better than he can—at sea!"

These were not exactly Aules Pulena's words, but Vel knew how pleased the old man would be to hear them. Ocno seemed thunderstruck by the news. First he was silent, then he gave a yell of joy, flung his leather cap into the air, and danced a jig on the deck like an old goat that had just taken leave of its senses. When he was out of breath he stopped and panted.

"The gods bless your father and let him see his great-grandchildren!" he cried. "Why, this is really something. Goat or no goat, I'm sure the voyage couldn't start under better auspices. That overdressed Greek of yours will have the time of his life with Tulumnes, who's so mad about everything Greek. And we'll have the time of our lives as well. And now, Felus," he called to the mate, "weigh anchor!" And he started up one of the sea chanties he had picked up in some harbor tavern along the Tyrrhenian coast.

Vel was delighted to be back in his cabin, with its fur-covered bunk, and this time to have it all to himself. The breeze blowing from inland took the two ships far from the shore and kept up all that day and the next night. Ocno raised all possible sail to keep up with the *Captain,* and with the wind behind them they flew across the waves, though the cargo was weighing them down a little. Very soon Vel felt himself completely at one with the rhythm of the ship; the deep water, only slightly agitated by the wind, swished vigorously around the *Boar*'s head, the oars motionless in their rowlocks, whistled in the wind, and the stretched ropes squeaked and groaned in the pulleys which the friction had made smooth and polished. All these sounds were familiar, and so was the wonderful salty wind and the wings of a solitary gull swooping white in a sky that grew steadily bluer as the day went on. Lying on a coil of rope with his knees higher than his head, Vel was luxuriating in sea and sky and gulls and breeze, and day dreaming.

In the afternoon he made the rounds of the *Boar,* to sniff his favorite smell of tar again, and popped down to the hold for a look at the cargo—"his" cargo. There, between the oarsmen's benches, he chatted for a while with the fat overseer, but maintained a cool distance, for he disliked the fellow with his rather bestial face with its small cruel eyes.

That evening, before going to bed, he spent a long time gazing at the stars, which were all that shone in the sky, for the new moon was still only the thinnest crescent. Ocno described the spring constellations, delighted with the following wind that was still carrying them along. Vel told him about the circus and the show. The old man smiled. "I was on land like you and at the circus just as you were—not in the gallery of course, but I was in the dressing room, and I can tell you there's no better place for judging a match, even before the athletes have set foot in the arena. And look here—my trip ashore was quite a profitable business, as well." And he

took a weapon that glimmered faintly out of his belt—
a short knife shaped like an olive leaf sharpened on
both sides with a bone handle about the same length as
the blade. Vel took it in his hand and from the weight
he knew it was made of the new material he had seen
in Velthur's workshop. It was perfectly balanced, too,
and easy to throw as well as a good sharp cutter.

"I won it off a silly overdressed young fool who was
keeping this wonder just for its looks—I swear it, on
this cap of mine—and tried making a bet with me. By
Poseidon, they know what to do with that iron of theirs
in Populonia, I must say!" And Ocno weighed the knife
in his hand, then poked it into the common pot where
the kid sacrificed that morning was steaming away—for
only the blood was given to the gods, the rest of course,
belonging to the priest who made the sacrifice, which,
on his own ship, meant Ocno. "It's not as if it's only for
picking up goat's meat with!" the old rascal concluded.
Vel felt properly at home as he followed Ocno's example and munched vigorously with the others. After supper, Felus and another man played dice in the faint red
glow of the stove, and Vel moved over to Ocno for his
lesson on the stars.

Next day about mid-morning they saw land on the
horizon—a bluish outline in the distance. The *Captain*
was no longer within call, but she was well in sight, less
than a single sea mile away, Ocno thought. They sped
after her, the sail still hoisted.

"A fine lazy life those oarsmen are leading," Ocno
grumbled, but only out of habit, for when the gods were

generous with this favorable wind, everyone profited from it. After the midday meal they were very close to the shore. Vel was surprised by the silence of the small bay where the *Captain* already rode at anchor, a silence disturbed only by the seagulls' cries and the waves breaking on the rocks. It was a very beautiful place covered with woods, but however hard he looked, Vel could see none of the lookout towers his father had told him about in Populonia. They disembarked very cautiously, prepared for any attack that might come—Ocno with his new knife, and Vel with a stout leather cap that Ocno made him ram down to his ears.

"Those shepherds can really throw stones—by hand or sling—and if you happen to get one on the head you'll thank me for that cap, lad," he told Vel, who protested at the discomfort of wearing what was really a tight sort of helmet. They met the *Captain*'s men already weighed down with a dozen large jars made of porous clay; these were water containers that were wrapped in straw and wedged firmly on wooden racks in the hold, and there kept the water cool and fresh for days. The bay consisted of a small sweep of very fine white sand less than two hundred paces across between the hostile sea, that threatened to swallow up the land, and the tough dark woods battered by the wind, seared by the salt spray, that put down roots wherever a crumb of earth could be found as a defense against the sea. Vel went across to his father, who was talking to Ocno.

"Let me go and get water with the others, Father," he said. "Please let me!"

Aules allowed himself to be persuaded. Two of his men and the mate knew just where to find the water, and guided the little group inland, through the woods. The further they went, the thicker grew the trees, fairly large pines and ilex oaks over an undergrowth of small, thorned bushes with blue or white flowers that turned into delicious blackberries in autumn. As the men moved cautiously ahead, slightly oppressed by the air of mystery aroused by the shade and the silence about them, even the birds were quiet. Vel was the first to shake off this uneasiness when he saw a small creature with a large tail climbing up the trunk of a pine tree and gazing at him with lively round eyes as soon as he was safe on a branch.

"Look, Ocno, a squirrel!" he yelled, and the old man jumped.

"May the gods of the woods protect you," Ocno grumbled. "There's no need to scream in my ear like that in this awful place!"

"Scared? If your old pirate friends could just see you!"

"Will you shut up! May a mermaid gobble you up! I've told you a thousand times I won't have that word. Don't you realize it's not safe to say it anywhere on this earth? And anyway, whoever told you I was . . . Anyway, you shouldn't listen to all the old wives' tales you hear. And it's true, I hate walking through the woods. Give me a new route, and whether the wind's favorable or not, I'm ready to try it—but creeping along through these thickets, under these great dark trees . . ."

"But there's no one here! Don't you see? Apart from the nymphs who live in tree trunks, there's no one at all. Look, I'm sure a nymph lives here!" And Vel poked at an oak all festooned with dark ivy whose gay flowering clusters looked like buds. But before Ocno could reply, the path, which had been sloping down for the last few minutes, opened out into a very green, mossy amphitheater made of rock and shaped like a shell, which echoed the gurgling sound of the fountain that arose, clear and sparking, almost in the middle of it. Obviously this was a sacred place, for it had been decorated and altered a little. In the place where the water gushed out of the rock, was a piece of oak tree bark shaped into a kind of cradle that collected the water and sent it into a stone basin. Here the water collected making a pool about as deep as the height of a man. Plants seemed to darken the bottom but when Vel peered over the rough edge of the basin he could see some tiny white stones at the bottom. He saw a garland of flowers, too, rocking over the small ripples made by the falling water. When his eyes had gotten used to the dimmed light of the place, he found a shelf cut out with some rough tool in the wall of rock on which stood two small loaves, a piece of cheese, and an earthenware plate with something brownish on it—honey perhaps.

One of the two sailors who had led the short march through the woods explained: "It's a very famous spring," he said. "I've been here twice before. There's no one along the coast who doesn't know of it. And the

people who live here"—he went on, raising his voice—
"are very hospitable to anyone who doesn't touch their
sacred offerings and doesn't profane the place. They
allow decent sailors with peaceful intentions to fill their
water jugs here and give thanks to the sacred nymph."
He almost shouted these last words.

"Why are you shouting like that?" Vel asked, surprised. But without answering, the man merely urged
his companions to hurry and fill their jugs. One man
climbed right up to the spout and filled the jugs, one at
a time, then passed them back to the others. Meanwhile
Vel was examining the place. He saw that the feet of
pilgrims who came to get water and honor the nymph
had made small paths that vanished into the wood, and
he was tempted to follow one of them. This would no
doubt have brought him to a village of the mysterious
shepherds his father had spoken of. Suddenly the squawk
of a magpie on a branch made him look up, and he
thought he saw movement behind one of the trees surrounding the place. But it vanished, and when he looked
again he saw nothing.

"Are there bears in these woods?" Vel asked the
sailor who had explained things a little earlier.

"Bears?" he repeated. "No, certainly not, sir. There
might be wolves perhaps, but not here in the woods; on
the plains inland on the pastures, that's where you find
them."

The water jugs were now full. The *Captain*'s mate
went up to the basin and took some brown grains and

an iron knife from his tunic and a small double-sided battle ax, the kind Vel had seen in the workshops of Populonia, from his belt.

"The noble merchant Aules Pulena of the Etruscan city of Tarquinia, wishes to give thanks to the generous nymph of this place with these grains of perfumed incense which I will burn in her honor, as people in the East do and my own people do also; and to the good people of this country with these stout weapons of solid bronze and well tempered iron."

He laid the ax and the knife on the edge of the basin, and the incense in a small cavity in the rock. A sailor came over carrying a stick and a small wooden table with a hole in it, twirled the stick around fast in the hole till it started to smoke, and finally lit a small flame. The incense burned slowly, with a powerful smell.

"I see," said Vel, lowering his voice without knowing why. "When the shepherds come to get water in a few hours they'll find father's gifts."

"In a few hours, or much sooner!" answered Ocno, as he picked up a dripping water jug. "Let's go, or your father will think one of your imaginary bears has eaten the lot of us."

They went back more slowly than they had come, laughing and joking as people do after feeling tense. Even Ocno seemed to like the woods better, and actually admired a magpie who flashed past on blue-black wings.

Vel ran up to his father, delightedly.

"Here we are, with the clearest water ever. We didn't

see a soul, but we left your presents for those shepherds."

"You didn't see anyone, eh? Well, you should have
looked behind the bushes and the trunks of those oak
trees," replied Aules, taking Vel by the shoulder and
twirling him around toward the wood he had just left.
"Look!"

To Vel's enormous surprise, seven or eight men and
two boys had appeared out of nowhere and now stood
still and silent among the bushes, apparently not in-
tending to come forward. They all carried stout sticks,
and three of them had leather slings flung over their
shoulders and a few round stones, as big as apples, bulg-
ing in a bag they carried at their belts. The oldest had
Aules' double-sided battle ax and another standing beside him, his son perhaps, had hung the iron knife on
a thin leather sling and was wearing it around his neck.
The group of sailors, standing stock still with astonishment on the beach, and the shepherds in the bushes,
stood staring in silence at each other for several sec-
onds. Then Aules Pulena moved a few steps toward
the shepherds, raising his hand in a gesture that meant
he wanted to speak. In a moment the men had vanished.

"Oh Father, why have they run away?" Vel cried.

"Who can tell? They're as timid as the wild creatures
of these woods. You see, they were curious to see us,
but they're not sociable and they're frightened of what
the sea may bring to their shores, as I told you."

"But they can defend themselves if they have to,"

muttered Ocno. "I wouldn't like to meet those sticks of theirs, and they seem pretty clever with those slings as well."

The sailors were climbing up the gangplank to stow away the water, and Aules went over to Ocno.

"From now on the *Boar* musn't lose sight of the *Captain*," he said. "If this favorable wind continues, we'll reduce sail. If it doesn't, then the *Boar*'s quite up to my ship, which has more oarsmen but more weight as well." He made no mention of the third possibility, which he knew perfectly well Ocno had in mind, just as he had.

"We'll streak after you like a shark after its prey," Ocno replied. "The route's still the one we agreed on, is it?"

"Of course. Sethre's a good helmsman and he says you agree. We go west from the island and simply follow the coastline in a curve as far as Massalia."

"I might have gone more directly myself, straighter across the sea, reaching Massalia from the south; but the two routes are much the same . . . when the gods of the abyss aren't too greedy, that is, and the gods of the air are resting in heaven."

Ocno stopped, seemed about to add more, and then shrugged and was silent. Aules Pulena had been watching him and had noticed the way his expression had changed.

"I think I know what you're thinking," Aules said, lowering his voice. "These last few days have been exceptionally good for early spring. And I saw the petrels flying south against the wind as well when we were still in Populonia." Ocno nodded.

"We'll keep in sight of each other, and for the rest trust in the gratitude of Poseidon, who took the blood of my kid, after all!"

Without saying goodbye to his son again, Aules Pulena resolutely turned his back on the *Boar* and hurried his men on. They embarked quickly and the two ships set sail. The *Boar* raised both sails, and the *Captain*, using only the mainsail, seemed to be holding back.

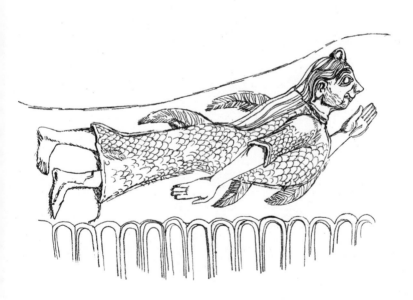

Bronze relief of a mermaid; 500 B.C.

VIII.

THE ANGER OF POSEIDON

The first days at sea went well but Vel was going through a bad time. He was lucky not to suffer from seasickness, and, in fact, he was perfectly comfortable with the smell of warm tar on the deck which felt so good under his feet. With Ocno's approval he had left his sandals in the cabin and now went barefoot.

"A real sailor has such hard soles to his feet that a nail won't pierce them. And the palms of his hands are just the same, so that the ropes don't take the skin off them," Ocno told him. No, the trouble had nothing to do with the rhythmical movement of the ship; Vel simply felt alone and homesick, and out of his element, devoured by some inner restlessness.

From dawn till sunset he was chased by orders from Ocno, Vipis, and Felus. He had to wash the deck, haul-

ing water up from the sea in a heavy bucket, first scrap-
ing into every corner with a currycomb; he had to help
the cooks clean the pots; work at the pulleys with the
others whenever they had to change direction or catch
the wind; climb up into the riggings, "or do any other
damned bit of hard work that comes into the old man's
wretched head!" Vel thought, exhausted. This he
thought but said nothing of, because once when he tried
to protest Ocno merely shrugged.

"Your father entrusted you to me," he said, "and I'm
a different sort of tutor from that old Greek of yours.
If you don't like it you can find another when we get
back to Tarquinia."

But after six days of the treatment, Vel realized that
all this tearing about had given his hands terrible blis-
ters that smarted and hurt him—but it had also taken
his mind off the sea, stretching endlessly around the
Boar, ready to change its mood at any moment and
crush the ship to pieces.

On the morning of the seventh day, Vel got up and
left the cabin feeling happy. He was delighted with the
fresh air and the *Captain*'s white sails not far away
astern, and by the rising sun, faintly veiled in silvery
mist.

"The gods are favoring us—they must have liked the
kid you sacrificed, Ocno," he said. "Look, here's another splendid day."

"Maybe next time I'd better sacrifice a ram or a pair
of oxen," grumbled Ocno. Vel looked at him with surprise.

"But isn't everything going well? Last night the sunset was fiery red, and you always said that's a good sign, didn't you?"

"No sign's so good that another can't cancel it out. If you'd been paying attention to what I've told you, you'd have realized the wind's changed!"

Vel knew he deserved this reproach. He licked his finger conscientiously, and held it up.

"Wind from the south," he said.

"Right. A damnable wind from the south." And without another word Ocno turned to the rudder. The *Boar* refused to stay on course and in order to keep the *Captain* in sight they they had to hoist the second sail. The sun rose, ringed by a strange greenish halo, and though the wind was not very strong, the billows, gray in the ghostly light, were swelling more and more and sending up plumes of white spray. But until evening nothing happened. The men gathered for supper and were on edge after the weary day spent sailing almost into the wind. Ocno, wanting the sailors to talk and so forget their tiredness, urged Vipis to tell them a story about his own country. Great black clouds had begun to gather, but the ceaseless south wind kept dispersing them, and sometimes they caught glimpses of the crescent moon, now slightly larger than when they had left Populonia. The oarsmen were huddled together in the hold, freed from the heavy chains that, as a rule, bound them to the oars, with lighter chains fixed to the walls which were long enough to let them lie down and turn over as they slept. But although they generally slept like logs the

Antefix;
6th-5th Century B.C.

moment they had finished their supper, tonight they lay awake, uneasy under that threatening sky, clanking their chains as they moved restlessly about talking together.

Vipis began his story, but Ocno soon realized it had not been a good idea, for the tale was dark and fearful to suit the threat that hung over them. He spoke of the forests in Campania, impenetrable stretches of oaks where wild boars and wolves were to be found; of woodland spirits who lived in tree trunks and bogs, and of mysterious caves where monsters roamed whom no one could describe, for no one had ever returned alive after seeing them. Furious at the effect this was having on the men, Ocno stormed at Vipis.

"By the demons of the abyss! Can't you talk about anything except these stupid old wives' tales? You'd better start the night watch right away and let the others go to sleep. Take the rudder, Vipis, and if you see a wild boar in the waves, apart from the ship's one, mind you, don't come and wake me! Take Siculo with you."

A sailor came forward. He was an excellent slave and as much at home at sea as he was in the slave quarters at Tarquinia; but silent and gloomy in character and looks.

"You won't get more than a grunt out of him," muttered Ocno. "So you can gossip away all you like!"

Vipis went off grumbling.

"I'll take over the second watch with Vel," Ocno called after him.

Vel lay down on his bunk, fully dressed, and pulled the soft, well-cured lambskin rug up to keep out the cold of the early spring night. At Tarquinia, he thought, his mother and old Ninia would never have let him do this; like every civilized person he would have had to undress.

"That's another good thing about living at sea," Vel said to himself, as he huddled happily under the skin, feeling at once shamefully dirty and marvelously snug. And with this thought, he fell fast asleep, forgetting the anxiety of the last few hours.

He woke up when he felt lifted off the bunk as if a gigantic hand had grabbed him and flung him across the floor brushing against the cabin door. Instinctively and desperately he tried to hold on to something solid, as the floor rose abruptly, and hurled him back towards the bunk. The cabin door broke open with a tremendous creaking, wrenched nearly off its hinges, and water burst in violently. Half blinded by the wave, which had caught him head on, Vel managed to crawl to the door, but it slammed again so hard that if it had hit him it would have smashed in his face. When at last, by leaning on it with his full weight, he managed to open it slightly and creep out, he found himself in the midst of a violent hurricane. "The storm!" he thought; and then, "How could I possibly have slept through all this row!" A strip of sail whistled down onto his back and made him jump: it was like a slap from a cold wet hand. The wind blew hot and sticky but with terrible violence, and the *Boar* danced on the waves, plunging down into what looked like snarling mouths. Beaten back to his cabin, soaked and half blinded by the water that slashed at him from every side, Vel had a moment of total terror that prevented him from thinking. The sound of people moving about was drowned by the whistling wind and the panting creak of the ship's wooden structure. Vel heard a sailor cursing, though he could not recognize the voice. He looked up toward the bow, trying to pierce the darkness. Ocno must be at the rudder, if there was still a rudder. For a long moment lightning broke the darkness, and his dazzled eyes saw the ship— its outline clearly visible, masts, rigging, deck, scrawled blackly, on his mind. He also saw a man pulling at the right hand stroke oar. It was Ocno!—only without his cap. With his head gleaming with water and his hair stuck to his cheeks, he was almost unrecognizable. Another flash showed Vel the biggest obstacles and the things he might cling to. He turned decisively to leave the cabin and a sudden heave from the *Boar*—which

reared up like a horse on its hind legs—rolled him over
on the floor. Somehow he must grab hold of the main
mast, only two steps away, or else the ship, hurtling
down again, would throw him into the bow, or even
overboard. When the wave came, he was ready for it,
hugging the mast which his arms could hardly get
around; he felt he was choking, plunging endlessly into
a salt whirlpool that filled his mouth and ears and
burned his eyes and made him afraid he would never
breathe again. The great cracks of thunder could only
be the voice of Aita, raging.

"This is the end," he thought, feeling strangely dull
and calm. "We'll all end up in Poseidon's kingdom."
Just then, he thought he saw a light. Yes, he could see
a small circle of soaking planks at his feet. It was the
lamp that burned in the hold at night, and the overseer
must have lighted it. From the hold came voices as well
as light, now that the thunder had left a trail of silence.
Vel realized the overseer was trying to free the oarsmen; he knew that in the case of storm or fire no captain
worthy of the name would let the slaves remain chained
to the oars. It was only in battle that they often per-
ished by going down with the ship. For a moment the
Boar seemed to right itself, becoming miraculously balanced. "Now or never!" thought Vel, and flung himself
forward, trying to use anything unmovable that came
to hand. Wearily he crawled a few yards, then the ship
heaved again and nearly flung him on top of Ocno. "By
all the gods in the abyss, get back to your cabin!"
yelled Ocno. "Why are you here? Haven't you seen

Felus? I sent him . . ." But Vel scarcely heard him. The last words were drowned by a fearful crunch as the main mast snapped off, a cubit from the bottom, and with a strangely slow fall crushed the *Boar* onto the deck. Relieved of its weight, the *Boar* listed heavily to port. Ocno dropped the stroke oar and grabbed at the ship's side. "Are we going down?" Vel shouted. The old man did not answer his question.

"We're only a few miles from the shore," he said. "Do you see? We've got to hang on till we get to the shore!"

"But how can we?" sobbed Vel, grabbing Ocno's arm.

"We've got to throw the mast into the sea right away." The words repeatedly shouted into Vel's ear, at last penetrated his brain. He looked around: a man was crawling laboriously toward them, and Vel could hear a chain rattling on the deck at each movement he made. Ocno realized it was one of the oarsmen and shouted to Vel: "The slaves?" Vel nodded, gesturing to explain that the overseer had broken the chains to gain time. Ocno made a sign that meant he had understood, grabbed the slave who had come up to them and took the hatchet he was carrying. The man looked at him and immediately looked back at the mast flung across the ship's side, which had broken where it had fallen. Without another word the three went over to the thick pinewood mast, and saw at once that it would be impossible to throw it into the sea as it was, jumbled up with the shrouds, weighed down with the sails. Ocno started belaboring the crossbeam with the hatchet, but with the ship's weight upset and the terrible waves lifting it up and then plunging it down, it was almost impossible to keep standing.

Two other sailors came up to help, and the mast was soon freed from its entanglements. In a row with infinite difficulty, they managed to lift the heavy end and slide it over the top of the ship's side. The men worked doggedly, panting, taking no notice of wind and water. There . . . the mast was now half overboard . . . for a brief moment it hung there, balanced and swaying . . . then it fell; and at that moment, a wave hit the side of the ship, which had so far been held down by the weight of the mast, and pushed it up with gigantic force; a mountain of water broke over it, sweeping everything away with it. Vel just had time to grab the cabin door, but it was only for a moment. Then he was dragged away, lifted and dropped into an abyss of black salty water that was trying to push into his nostrils, his mouth, his ears. He fell, grabbing desperately at the useless door, and came up again ten yards from the ship. In the light of its lamps, the *Boar* looked black and enormous, lost forever; Vel's ears buzzed, he had no will left to hold out. The heavy cabin door was holding him up, but, as the waves were beating on it, against the wind, it might fling him off at any moment. Vel gathered his final strength, and, hardly conscious, wretched and exhausted as a cat fallen into a well, managed to climb onto it and lie on his stomach, legs and arms flung out, hands clutching the edges. Then he fell into a kind of delirium, in which he was insensible to the fury of the storm and to everything else, too exhausted to keep suffering or to notice the passing of time. The fact that he was some way from the shore saved him, because the storm had time to wear itself out before morning. Had he been flung onto the beach that night, he would have been smashed on the rocks. Instead, the first light of dawn found him about a hundred yards from the shore where the waves were playing quietly, frilling around the sharp black rocks that encircled a small bay.

Vel heard them, but did not realize he was safe. When the door was flung against a rock, throwing him off it, he found himself in water up to his knees, and peering with swollen, burning eyes, saw a stretch of very white pebbly sand glittering in the bright morning. He was just able to drag himself to safety; then he fell on the ground and slept.

IX.

THE SIMPLE LIFE

When he awoke from his heavy dreamless slumber, still blind, still not realizing what was around him, Vel's eyes wandered from a wall made of round polished stones and pieces of rock to some small dried fish hanging on a line from the ceiling. Then he shut his dazzled eyes against a bright blue eye in the seaweed roof—a patch of sky. Slowly consciousness returned, and Vel started up from the bed, but fell back at once, groaning. Pain shot through his right leg, and his lips felt parched and swollen. A small figure who had so far been squatting beside the couch leaped up and ran over to the door of the hut, lifted a kind of curtain made of rushes, and dashed outside, calling. His shrill cries sounded to Vel like those of a seabird—not a word he said was understandable.

He was in an almost circular stone-walled hut. The opening in the roof must have been a chimney, because the rough hearth was right underneath it—simply a hole full of ashes. As he was looking around, the rush curtain was pulled abruptly aside and three or four boys of about his own age, a woman, and two men were brought in by the boy who had dashed out and was now pointing him out triumphantly to the others, talking without a pause and waving his hands. The others were silent. At first Vel felt so scared that tears rolled down his cheeks. Then the woman came up to him, holding out her hands and smiling: she was carrying a small gourd and held it out to him. Vel drank greedily and the sweet liquid slipped down his throat, feeling cooler than any drink he had ever had before. He smiled at the woman, who looked at him, took the gourd, and started to laugh loudly. Vel said, "Thank you, oh thank you! You're very kind. But where am I? Can you tell me where I am?"

At the sound of these words, the boys moved abruptly away and watched him from a safe distance. The woman shook her head, obviously not understanding. Finally one of the men, who wore a worn strip of wool around his long hair, seemed to have an idea. He chattered excitedly to another man in his own language, pointing first at Vel, then outside the door. The other man listened, then nodded vigorously, and both of them held out their hands as if telling Vel to wait. They then ran outside. The woman and the children stayed near him, staring at him with their black eyes and smiling broadly, till a man who looked very different from the others came into the hut. He was tall, with hair of an odd wheat color down to his shoulders, a moustache that merged with an untrimmed beard, and muscular arms and legs; the legs were wrapped in some peculiar garment that might have been trousers, but these were not full, like those the Persians wore, but tight and crisscrossed with laces from knee to ankle. Vel knew that not everyone had black eyes and hair, like the Greeks and the Etruscans; he knew that people in the north were oddly colored, for Ibico had described them, but he had never seen such fair skin, freckled with little golden specks, and blue eyes that hardly seemed real. But they were very friendly eyes, and the words that came through the strange man's long whiskers were Greek—a rather odd, disjointed Greek, that nevertheless made poor Vel's heart swell with relief.

"Are you Greek?" the fair giant asked.

"No, I am Etruscan," answered Vel, wondering what effect this would have on the man, and whether he was a friend of the Etruscans or an enemy.

"Do you come from that big, distant island the Greeks call Sardinia?"

"No, no." Vel realized the man simply did not know the name Etruscan. He tried to explain where he came from, speaking as clearly as he could. The giant seized on the word "ship" and shook his head.

"Your ship was broken on the rocks; our rocks are very bad for ships. I think only you and the old sailor were saved."

All Vel understood properly was the word "old" and,

taking no notice of his newly injured leg, he sprang to his knees on the bed and seized the man's arm.

"Who, who was saved? Where is he?"

The man understood Vel's anxiety, and reassured him with a smile. He turned to the woman, spoke as if he were giving her an order, and without a word she left the hut. Waiting was almost unbearable. Someone had been saved from that terrible wreck—but who? An old man. But there were at least four men on the *Boar* who seemed old to his eyes, not counting the slaves and their overseer. But the thought of the *Boar* reminded him of the *Captain*. What had happened to his father and the fine three-masted ship that was the Pulenas' pride? The fair man shook his head at Vel's question and raised a single finger. The wreck of just a single ship had been found on the rocks, he knew nothing about a second. Vel fell back on the bed, weak with despair. What hope was there that the *Captain* had been saved. Even the thought that someone had survived from his own ship did nothing to cheer him. He covered his head with a piece of his torn tunic, and, sitting on the bed, wept bitterly, weeping out all his suffering and all his weariness, till a familiar voice, a voice he felt he could not possibly be hearing, penetrated the depths of his despair.

"The gods be thanked a thousand times! So it really is my master's son! Vel it's you, it's you! So you're safe, my child!"

Vel peered incredulously out from behind his tunic to stare at Ocno's gray head pressing against his knees. So the old helmsman had really escaped the fury of the sea once again!

"So it really was you!" Vel cried. "Why, I should have known at once! Of course it was you!"

The people there watched the scene kindly. Other dark figures appeared in the doorway, asked for explanations, and pushed in to see. Clearly this was all very new in their simple existence.

But as soon as the joy of meeting was over, the two survivors were weighed down with sadness. At first, Vel dared not ask, but finally he came out with it.

"You're the only one, aren't you? All the others are dead."

Ocno hung his head: "I thought these people had found no one but me on the rocks; they answered my questions in a language I didn't understand. And then a tall fair man who speaks Greek came and told me about you." He shook his fist at the sky. "The gods are sometimes unjust and cruel! They've left me, and I'm old, whereas my beautiful *Boar* . . . and all my comrades . . . even Vipis and Felus . . . all, all are in the belly of Poseidon. Hungry monster!" Terrified, Vel put a hand over his mouth.

"Will you keep quiet!" he murmured. "Don't you think they've done enough, in their rage?" And the old man hung his head and was silent. Neither of them had mentioned the *Captain,* but the thought of the three-masted ship breaking up on the rocks and being swallowed piecemeal by the waves lay between them.

Ocno was the first to shake off his depression.

"But you're safe, Vel, that's what matters. Is anything wrong? Are you all right?"

"My leg hurts. I must have injured it on the rocks."

The old man examined it and Vel saw that a few rags were fastened to his knee, soaked in some green ointment that must have been made from boiled herbs.

"They've been looking after you, you see," said Ocno. "It may not be too bad and may soon disappear. We've been very lucky." He lowered his voice and went on in the thickest Tarquinian dialect, with a caution Vel thought excessive. "I've heard of native tribes who build their miserable huts among the rocks and during storms light lamps there, so that ships think there's a safe landing place and try to land. Afterwards these people fish out the wreckage thrown up on the rocks, and if there are any survivors . . ."

Ocno drew his hand across his throat in an expressive gesture. Vel's eyes opened wide.

"But these are kind, gentle fishermen," he went on. "Now, as soon as you're better, we'll have to find some means of transport to Massalia. We may not be far from it—about a hundred sea miles, if I've got my bearings right. The *Captain* must be on its way there and we must join her. Aules Pulena must hear that his man has lost the ship entrusted to him, but didn't die with her, as he should have done. But I swear, by all the gods . . ."

Vel did not allow him to finish.

"I'll tell my father what you did for the ship and for me. You're not to blame for the anger of the sea gods."

But Ocno leaped up at once. "I'm not afraid of the

gods, apart from the implacable Aita. And we haven't reached his underworld kingdom yet." He turned to the fair giant and to Vel's surprise the two men seemed to understand each other's language, helped by expressive gestures and grimaces, very much better than he and the giant had managed to. Reassured by old Ocno's survival, he felt hope returning. One of the children was staring at his right hand, and Vel knew why. The Pulena ring with the leopards on it, now his whole fortune, was still on his finger, and when he felt under his tunic he found the leather purse with his mother's coins still hanging on his belt. This discovery reassured him too, and even the pain in his leg seemed less bad. Yes, the gods were capricious and indifferent to human suffering; but he was Vel the Etruscan, no longer a boy but a man who had looked death in the face and escaped it.

Vel's leg had been seriously injured when the wave flung him onto the rocks. For the first two days during his long sleep, he had been delirious and feverish, and the woman who had cared for him kept changing the herbal remedies on his wound which the tribe's "wise man" prepared. But the herbs had had no effect. The wound had certainly healed, but underneath the skin the blood was flowing hotly and the flesh was inflamed, and Vel felt the pain piercing his very bones. Ocno scarcely left him, except for mysterious expeditions that kept him away for several hours around the middle of the day. But Vel was too tired to ask questions. He had become melancholy, and at night, though the sea had grown calm and the sky glowed with stars, he could not sleep and kept shifting about, making the pain worse. Six days after the shipwreck Vel had seen nothing of the village except the patch of beach he could see through the doorway. His leg was swollen and very painful and he kept wanting to cry but swallowed down the tears. Ocno came in with the fair man whose name Vel now knew was Ermor, and who came from a large nomad tribe inland; how he had come to the shores of the Great Sea, nobody knew. Anyway, he knew a little Greek, the mixture of dialects spoken around the coasts and known to sailors at least around the whole Mediterranean. And he knew Massalia. For these reasons Ocno had made a friend of him and they seemed to be getting along famously.

"The gods protect you, lad," Ocno greeted Vel, "and may your guardian spirit cure your body better than that skinny old wizard's done with his herbs. Let me see, now," and he took the bandage of moist herbs off and examined the leg with Ermor, looking anxious. Then, with a smile, he straightened up decisively.

"My master, son of Aules Pulena," he began very solemnly. Vel looked at him astonished, his fear and pain immediately growing.

"Am I going to die, Ocno? Tell me if I am. I want to know!"

The old man did not trouble to reassure him.

"You're enough of a man to choose for yourself. I've seen others with swollen limbs and this unlucky red color. Your blood is sick, and if we don't get it out quickly so as to release the evil spirits troubling you,

you really will die. But if we cut you and make a small opening for the sick blood to come through, then you'll get better, I'm quite sure."

"Cut me? But how?" Vel was terrified.

Ocno smiled.

"I knew you were brave, lad. Look!"

Vel, who had not meant to accept at all, was surprised at the old man's confidence and realized he could not draw back. And then, what Ocno was showing him was enough to take his mind off things. From the leather bag he carried at his helmsman's belt he had taken two beautiful iron razors which, Vel remembered, had been part of the cargo on the *Boar*.

"Then . . . the *Boar*?" he stammered, overwhelmed.

Ocno shook his head.

"No, the *Boar*'s lost; the waves are carrying what's left of the hull away, bit by bit. But these last few days Ermor and I and a couple of other fisherman have swum out to what the sea has left us of the wreck. And we managed to salvage a few things."

Vel fell back on the couch. He had hoped . . . well, that the *Boar* could still be recovered. Ah, if only he could get to Massalia with the cargo and the ship, damaged but safe! Then he thought bitterly how stupid he had been. How could he and Ocno, and old man and a wounded boy, manage the ship, even if it had been saved? Ermor had picked up one of the razors meanwhile, and was examining it carefully, trying out its edge with his thumbnail. Vel shook himself.

"Now I see where you've been these last few days,

when you weren't with me. If you want to cut off my leg, I'm ready. I know you'll do all you can to save me."

The old man seemed touched, but lost no more time talking. Ermor was sent to call the tribe's wise man, for Ocno was far too astute to do anything without flattering the "medicine man" by asking his advice.

When the wise man arrived, he left the train of women and children who followed him whenever he came through the village at the door. He was an old man, small and skinny and sunburned even in the deep wrinkles that covered his face, but his pale eyes gleamed with strange serenity, though the edges of their lids were red; his clothes were very simple, and only a necklace of polished sharks' teeth indicated his rank. He greeted them kindly, but all Vel could understand was the gentleness of his smile. Ocno, uninhibited as ever, tried to make himself understood, but had to ask Ermor to help him, and a very odd three-sided conversation took place, which Vel followed with great interest.

"May the gods protect the sage!" Ocno began, looking extremely respectful. "Yes, indeed, the boy and I are very grateful for your herbs—which are perfectly useless. I'm certain the leg will never be cured with that filthy poultice on it, Ermor, but don't tell him that, will you? Tell him we need some powerful spells and his help as a surgeon. Do you really think the old crab doesn't understand a word? Yes, yes, *spells—surgeon—* make him understand that!"

The wizard was listening attentively, staring at Ocno's face as he brought out compliments and insults with

exactly the same expression and tone and Ermor repeated only the compliments in the local language. At
the end of it all the medicine man went over to the
couch and uncovered Vel's leg. For a long time he
looked at the reddened flesh and then, moving very
suddenly, pressed his finger near the wound. Vel shrieked
and Ocno leaped up threateningly. But the old man
pointed to the white mark his finger had made, which
was slowly going back to its original color, and then
turned to Ermor and spoke slowly and solemnly for
several minutes.

"He says," said the painstaking interpreter, "that the
old mullet's right. Many evil spirits are weighing on the
child's leg and must be let out. They must be let out
with a knife, and he, Hoiarn, the medicine man, must
be ready beside the wound to capture them as they come
out and bind them with magic words to stop them from
spreading through the air and coming back to invade
another poor body. And he must put a spell on the
knife," he added, hurriedly translating the old man's
words.

Ocno turned red.

"Old mullet, eh? Well, I'm not arguing with a mad
barbarian. And the best spell you can put on a surgeon's
knife is the fire that makes it red-hot!"

The medicine man started talking to Ermor again
and Ermor translated.

"The sage says the genii of the fire will put a spell
on the knife and the herbs he'll give you to put on the
wound will stop the boy's blood—the good blood that

is—so that it won't escape and take the spirits of life away with it."

In spite of his anxiety, Vel could not help smiling.

"You see, Ocno, the old crab's not so stupid; in fact I'd say he understands the old mullet's thoughts even before Ermor speaks to him. The way the fishes understand each other, I suppose." Then he turned to Ermor again. "Will you ask him when my leg's going to be cut? I *must* get well soon, do you see? I *must* be able to walk again." And he fell back on the couch, exhausted.

Hoiarn listened to the boy's excited words, then laid a hand on his head, a dry, warm, light hand that was strangely comforting. He spoke to the interpreter but never stopped looking very kindly at Vel.

"Tomorrow at dawn, when you're rested, my son," Ermor translated. "And when your stomach is empty and your spirit ready. But do not fear, none of the evil genii that live in your leg can resist the curses of Hoiarn. He will leave you now with the old man who loves you like a father and will go up the hill, to the great oaks where he must seek the healing herbs the forest maidens will show him. Many of the sacred maidens who live in the old tree trunks and fountains of the woods are friends of Hoiarn, the medicine man."

And the old man made a dignified exit, with his small train falling reverently into line behind him, and Ermor followed.

Ocno had stood there stupified; but he shook himself and burst out laughing. "By the mermaid that suckled my grandfather! That cunning old rascal knows all the rules of medical art, and knows them well! An empty stomach, a spirit that's ready! I'd like to hear what our sophisticated doctors in Tarquinia would have to say about him, who won't move a step without a flask of Campanian wine. But what he said about the sacred maidens—oh, by Poseidon, I can't swallow that!"

Vel interrupted him.

"Don't mock the gods, Ocno, are you mad? And gods you don't know, at that. Think of my leg."

"You're right, you're right! The egg's got more sense than the cock, and that's a fact. Watch me, now!"

Ocno made a number of magical gestures and spat on the floor three times to scatter the bad luck his imprudent laughter might have drawn down on him. When he was quite reassured, he squatted down on the earth floor beside the couch.

"And now," he said, "I've got some news that'll make you happy, my fine lad! The *Boar*'s done with, it's true —but we're not entirely without resources. And meantime, we've got a boat!"

"A boat?" Vel shot up in bed.

"No, no, if you don't keep calm I won't tell you a thing. That's right, lie down like that. All this time I've been trading—and I can tell you, lad, that when Ocno trades, his Tyrrhenian blood really comes out—though he may not have the Pulena leopards glittering on his finger. And quite a number of sharks, even in Greece itself, may have found themselves pretty badly done in. But these people are honest and good, and I haven't cheated them,"—he added hastily when he saw Vel suddenly frowning—"in fact I've been generous, I really have. Anyway, you'll see!"

"What's left of the cargo?"

"Not much, I'm afraid. But a good many knives, saws, and tools. And that's all terribly valuable to these people, who often do carpentry with tools we'd laugh at. Do you know that at Massalia they still haven't gotten that new metal from the island of Elba, that iron stuff? So Ermor said. The *Captain* will do wonderful business if . . ." and he stopped himself, biting his lips.

"If Poseidon hasn't swallowed her up!" Vel concluded, turning his head away, because his eyes were suddenly pricking.

"What an old fool I am! Curse my chattering old tongue! The Greeks should have cut off a slice of it. But you must believe me, son. I'm sure—do you realize, *sure*—that Aules Pulena has saved the *Captain*. We weren't far from each other in the storm and there were no wrecks along this coast for several miles. For three days I've been sailing along them, trying out the boat."

Vel looked at him, filled with hope.

"You really haven't seen anything? Not a bit of the keel or the mast or . . ."

"Nothing, I tell you. When our tortoise takes us to Massalia, we'll find your father with the *Captain*, and all her cargo sold so well he won't mind having lost the *Boar*. You'll see."

For Vel, the day passed quickly. Ocno left him only for a few minutes and they never spoke of his leg; instead, they discussed every detail of the voyage to

Massalia. Only one difficulty worried Ocno. How could they get to Massalia alone, an old man and a boy who was still weak and unable to get around properly? Ocno said that with enough provisions and favorable winds he would be prepared to go as far as Sicily, but Vel was a good deal less optimistic. Perhaps it was partly because of the pain in his leg, which grew worse toward evening. The night passed between wakefulness and dozes in which he had strange, fearful dreams. When dawn finally came and the hut was filled with a milky light, poor Vel had been lying awake, scared, for some hours.

The wise man arrived, accompanied by Ocno and Ermor, only when it was fully day. The excited train of followers stayed respectfully outside the door, but every now and then friendly, worried faces peeped through the reed curtain for a moment and then withdrew. Camuloghna, the kind woman Vel remembered had always smiled as she made him swallow spicy, aromatic fish soups, was busy on her knees at the earth hearth in the middle of the room, fanning the fire.

Hoiarn signaled her to stay there and, before going over to Vel's couch, gave her some orders. She then went out with out with an earthenware bowl, to fetch water.

"How are you?" asked Ocno, and he went straight on, without further ado. "The old crab here's talking about tying you up and other nonsense like that. I told him a boy who's been at sea with me and lived through such a storm isn't a spoiled brat from a rich home, but a sailor, a true sailor. There's no need to tie you, like a girl who's scared of having a tooth out. You're not afraid of a little thing like this, are you?"

"No," answered Vel, reluctantly, "no, not if you're with me." Ocno had a damnable way of answering his own questions that forced Vel to put a bold front on it, so as not to lose face, but the cold sweat was starting up on his forehead and he could not help following old Hoiarn's movements through half-shut eyes. How was it that he had failed to notice how menacing the old leathery face was? Or was he wrong? Was it just that today his fear made everything look horrible?

Hoiarn was kneeling by the fire, which crackled up, flinging sparks up to the hole in the roof. The flames lit up his face and Vel realized that he had painted himself with clay stripes that gave him a pretty alarming appearance. He would have liked to ask Ermor what these stripes meant, but did not dare. The old man held his thin hands to the fire, and, throwing back his head, started intoning in a shrill, high voice: it sounded like invocations, threats, or prayers.

Though he did not understand a word, when the old man hid his shaggy white head in his arms Vel guessed that some of it must be names of divinities. Camuloghna had returned with the bowl overflowing, but out of respect and fear had stopped in the doorway. Suddenly Hoiarn stopped his invocations and flung a handful of blackish dried herbs on to the flames. A thick, strongly-smelling cloud rose from the hearth, and the herbs must have had a slightly hypnotic effect, because quite soon the smoke made Vel's head swim, though he still watched what was going on through half-shut lids, seeing the figures around him more and more confusedly. Perhaps it was his weakness that made everything seem to wave and float before him. The only real, solid thing was Ocno's arm, which he squeezed tighter and tighter.

He saw Camuloghna slip off at a gesture from Ermor, and come back with a full pan which she put on the flames in a corner of the hearth. He saw the old man take a bronze razor from his leather pouch, and in spite of his dazed condition, thought how Ocno must have given it to him as a present. While Hoiarn repeated his shrill invocations and made a number of deep bows, he kept passing the razor through the flames. Vel felt Ocno holding his shoulders, and a sense of relief when the leg was cleaned with steaming cloths taken from the pan; then he felt a weight on his ankles, which meant Ermor's strong hands were holding them tightly but not hard, while the giant stood smiling at him. Vel shut his eyes, concentrating desperately on the effort not to cry out, and when the razor cut him he shrieked just once. Then he felt something warm flowing on his leg, and at the same time a feeling of relief, as if the tension that had held his muscles stiff had suddenly slackened. He opened his eyes. The old medicine man was pressing the open wound, from which black blood mixed with pus was pouring out in a great stream. Vel stared at it, fascinated. Now the bad blood, and with it the evil spirits that had been tormenting him for so many days, would all be gone.

"Did you see?" he said, turning to Ocno. "I wasn't frightened. You didn't really believe I wouldn't yell, did you? Just once, that doesn't count!" And he fainted. But what stayed in his mind was the incredible sight of Ocno's contorted face, with a suspicious gleam in his small shark's eyes, just as if the old pirate was going to weep!

Vel's wound took another two weeks to heal, and left him with a white scar where the burning knife had cut him. He hoped it would never disappear, so that he could show it to prove his terrible adventure. After all, it was almost a war wound! But at the end of the first week he had already regained his strength and could limp to the shore with the help of Camuloghna's son Hencar, who had become a great friend. From him Vel had learned a number of words in the village dialect, and Hencar conscientiously repeated the Etruscan words Vel taught him. But gradually, as he became stronger, Vel grew more and more restless, and spent his time badgering Ocno to settle the day of their departure. Both his entreaties and his anger completely failed to shift the old man, who merely shrugged.

"I don't intend to take you back to your father half dead with the fever you'd catch after the first day at sea. Besides, I need healthy people on board. I can't do it all myself." This admission, which cost the old helmsman a good deal to make, persuaded Vel for a few hours; then he started up again. At last he found an entirely unexpected ally. One evening at sunset, on the eighteenth day after his operation, he was sulking on the beach, gazing at the new *Boar*. This was what Ocno had wanted to call the miserable tub he had bought, fixed up and given a kind of sail, helped by the taciturn, yet able Ermor.

"The spirit of the old *Boar*," he explained to Vel, "will be condemned to wander without form forever, unless we call it to dwell in our new boat. It's a fine, brave spirit, and there aren't many to match it on the Great Sea."

So the broad, clumsy craft lying low in the water had been called the *Blue Boar*, although it had no boar's head on its prow like the old ship. Vel sat leaning against it with his legs in the sand, worried, and deep in thought, when a shadow stopped in front of him.

"Hallo, boy," said a deep voice. "You seem sad this evening, as if your evil spirits had taken over again."

It was Ermor, who had come up silently. Vel shrugged.

"If that pig-headed old fellow didn't insist on waiting, we could be at sea by now. And it's all because of my leg, which doesn't even hurt any more." Ermor smiled.

"Then you can stop worrying. We're leaving at dawn tomorrow."

"What! Did you say *we're* leaving? Are you coming with us?" Vel was astounded. "But I can't take you into my service; I may not have anything, a father or riches . . ."

"Did I ask you for anything, *sir?*" Ermor grunted menacingly.

"Oh no! I didn't mean that, I didn't mean to offend

you—you know you're my friend," Vel explained hurriedly. "But you had no intention of going to Massalia and you mustn't come just for me . . . that is, for us!"

"The intentions of men are as changeable as the spring winds," said Ermor. "Anyway, I'm a Celt and Celts are vagabonds—they don't like staying in the one place for long. And I like Massalia. The old man is my friend, and besides, who can stop Ermor against his will? I have neither women nor children who hold a man down more firmly than anchors made of bronze. I will come to Massalia with you."

And without another word he walked away, after what was a very long speech indeed, considering his temperament. Anyway, Vel was too delighted to ask any more questions. As soon as he could, he went back to Camuloghna's house and found her in the one general room where the fire was always alight, and where he had been sleeping all this time. She greeted him with a kind smile but without a word, and Vel realized she had heard the news of their departure already and was sad. Shortly afterwards, others began to come in from the village, men, women, and children, all friends of Vel and in particular of Ocno, who had become extremely popular during his short stay there. The old fishermen warmed to him because of his knowledge of the sea, and the boys simply got along well with him and loved his stories. Besides, most families in the village had been enriched by something recovered from the *Boar*'s cargo. The medicine man was particularly proud of his new razors, which were spreading his fame as a remarkable surgeon throughout the surrounding villages. A gleaming bronze tool was very rare and iron quite unknown. So the farewells went on far into the night. When everyone had left at last, Vel drew Hencar aside. Now that he was really off, his thoughts were full of his father and the *Captain* and Massalia, yet he had a strange pain in his heart at the thought of never seeing his benefactors again.

"Come with me and Ocno, Hencar," he suggested. "You could become a fine sailor on one of our ships, and you'll always be my friend. My father"—he swallowed the lump he always felt in his throat when he said these words—"my father will be eternally grateful for what you and your family have done for me. And as for mother, why, she's so beautiful and so good, and we'd have a wonderful time in Tarquinia!"

Hencar shook his head.

"I'm sad that you are going away across the sea, my friend. But, as you know, I am the only one to get fish for my mother and sisters, since my father failed to come back from the sea so many moons ago. You'll come back again some day and I will welcome you to my house, and perhaps you will see my children, for I shall be a fisherman like my father and shall always live here. Now I salute you, and may all the gods of the waves be propitious to you and favorable winds swell your sail. Tomorrow morning we shall not see each other, because when you leave I shall already be out at sea fishing." Vel jumped up and held his right arm out horizontally, while he touched his forehead with his left hand. This

was the way the Etruscan people of Tarquinia bade a solemn farewell when they were going away for a long time from someone dear to them, and when they were saying goodbye forever, as well. Hencar said nothing, but tried to imitate him. Then the two boys hugged each other hard, and Hencar was the first to pull away and ran to hide his sorrow in the next room, the only other in the house.

That night Vel slept the deep, refreshing, dreamless sleep he had not slept for a very long time.

X.

AT SEA

Through the misty clouds on the horizon the sun peered, glittering on the water, and the square, patched sail of the new *Blue Boar* bellied gloriously in the following wind. The boat was very primitive. Ocno had made her out of a simple punt-like rowing boat on the beach. For days he had worked furiously to stop up the cracks with tar, to make the rudder secure, to reinforce the sides with planks of fir wood, which he managed to curve by treating them with water, and finally to set up a small mast that would hold the sail without upsetting the balance of the boat.

Ermor had not often been to sea, and never more than a few miles out, helping the village fishermen.

"Do you think your boat will keep up if the wind grows stronger?" he now asked Ocno, as he moved cau-

Wall painting;
6th Century B.C.

tiously to port because the boat was listing slightly to starboard. Ocno gave him a mischievous glance from under his thick eyebrows.

"Well! I doubt it! If the wind blows hard I think we'll just have to creep along the shore and wait for it to drop."

The new *Boar* was sailing near a coast that grew steadily rockier. Black rocks stuck up out of the sea from small glittering crescent-shaped beaches, pebbly but sandless.

"The coast is all like this as far as Massalia," said Ermor. "I've been along it on land, riding, but I never left the sea and always saw these rocks. Endless stones, and no trees—just this undergrowth"—and he gestured at the thick dark wood that clung obstinately to the thin soil and made a kind of curly black beard around the stony shore.

"How long did it take you to get from the village to Massalia on horseback?" Ocno repeated the question for Vel's benefit, because he had already questioned Ermor closely about it.

"I didn't push myself and didn't travel at night; I took things easy. The sun had just risen for the fourth time when I reached the outskirts, where the first houses are. Massalia's a big city and its port is like a crescent with two ends. We arrived at the eastern end."

"Three days on horseback, and no nights," Ocno murmured aloud. "And taking it easy. If the wind's any help my sail's a lot better than a horse, however different the new *Boar* is from the old one. At dawn the third day from now we should see the port, at latest. Ah, when I think we should have been there three weeks ago, and with our cargo intact! If the gods have any shame at all, they should take us to Massalia without our having to touch the oars. But those who sit on the clouds or in the coral palaces in the depths of the sea don't lend much of an ear to the prayers of poor mortals!"

Vel shook his head, smiling.

"Then you wasted the two doves whose blood is still staining the prow!" he said.

"What strange people you are," said Ermor gravely. "Your lack of respect for your gods is really extraordinary. How can you honor them and at the same time insult them? You make the right sacrifices, but if they don't listen to you, you dare to speak scornfully of them. How can you even raise your eyes to the terrible ones? All man can do is bow to their will and hope his actions will not offend them."

Vel was astonished at Ermor's loquacity. He tried to explain his point of view, picking his words carefully, because he too had sometimes tried to answer the questions that lurked in his mind.

"We Etruscans know the gods are great and terrible, and watch our small destinies from a great distance. But what's also true is that man somehow participates in the divine nature as well. He isn't like my cat that died or like, say, a calf—creatures whose lives are over, after this one. And some of the gods are friends of man, and catch him in their arms and carry him on their great wings to the divine banquet."

"Yes, that's what the soothsayers say, I've heard them with my own ears, though I'm a sailor and not much of a one for the divine," said Ocno. "But that's not what your Greek tutor believes. A hundred times I've seen him sneering at our superstitions!"

"The Greeks don't believe in genii, or things like that," said Vel, who, since Ibico had been left behind in Populonia, had felt generous towards him, and had been ready to defend him, "but they believe in Hades, because they put the shades of their heroes there, and Zeus rules the destinies of men, after all. But I believe every people honors the gods in a different way, and I think that's quite right. For instance, it would be silly to sneer at Camuloghna for thinking the shark that swallowed her husband was a god."

"If you get any wiser I don't think the *Boar* will stand it—it'll sink like a stone. And I don't think you're so full of wisdom that you'll refuse a modest meal when I get it out of that knapsack."

After Vel had eaten two wheatcakes, a few small fishes dried in the sun, and a dozen root vegetables cooked in hot ashes, and had drunk some goat's milk, Ocno felt reassured that his wisdom had not yet taken away his appetite.

Next day they sailed smoothly ahead and nothing new had happened by the evening, when a glowing red sunset promised another splendid spring day. The *Boar* had been making good progress in the wind that kept blowing from the east, and now the three of them lay down in the bottom of the boat, under Ermor's goatskin rug, the rough rudder secured to keep them on course. Ocno was very pleased with the new member of the crew. That morning the sea had been choppy, and the *Boar* had rocked uncomfortably, but Ermor had taken it like a sailor. Vel stared up at the stars, trying to remember the names of the constellations that Ibico had shown him—the Fishes, Castor and Pollux, Aries, Orion, the Bear. His watch was to be at dawn, but when some salt water spraying over him made him open his eyes, he realized right away that Ocno had let him sleep on, in fact that he had pulled the goatskin up over his face to keep the light from waking him. The sun had not yet risen from the sea, but the sky was already light.

"It's my watch!" Vel shouted crossly. So Ocno was treating him like a soft little girl, was he? Or was it that he didn't trust him with the boat's safety? He leaped up and almost tumbled back into the bottom when the *Boar* swerved suddenly. But at that very moment the boat emerged from the shadow of a creek and turned around a small promontory, and Vel was silent, for before him, like a wide amphitheater, lay the port of Massalia with three small islands forming a kind of natural barrier to it. Vel hung onto the mast, seeing nothing around him and staring at the anchorage so hard that his eyes were burning. All kinds of craft of all sizes were lined up a few yards from the shore, tugging at their anchor chains in the transparent water. He could see them all clearly, and the rowing boats and rafts for carrying cargo that swarmed about them. But where was the *Captain?* No three-masted ship appeared among the others—nothing— . . . Then a hoarse cry broke through his desperation and Ocno's hard fingers bit into his arm.

"There, on the shore, in that dock behind the quay there—look, it's the *Captain!*"

Then Vel saw her. He could not have recognized her before. The Pulenas' proud ship looked like a great grounded whale, with no masts at all except the smallest. But sailors and carpenters were busy on deck under the orders of a tall man whose white cloak Vel knew so well; and when he saw him joy, relief and excitement made him nearly fall into Ocno's arms. But Ocno shouted to Ermor and flung Vel at him like a bale of merchandise.

"By Poseidon's trumpet, are we going to be ship-wrecked right here in the harbor of Massalia?" he yelled, and flung himself on the rudder to avoid a collision with a large boat laden with sawn tree trunks, coming peacefully out of the harbor. Vel helped Ocno strike the sail and seized a pair of oars. Ermor did the same, and Ocno cautiously managed the rudder to avoid any other ships that might be setting sail. It was not like landing in Populonia; here, no one seemed to bother about them. Obviously a boat's arrival in this large Greek port was not of the smallest interest. It took them over a half an hour to reach the *Captain,* and a few yards away from it Vel dropped the oars, no longer caring about keeping the balance, and suddenly leaped into the bow and started waving his arms wildly and shouting his father's name. At first the noise of hammers and the creaking of a great windlass that was raising the main mast drowned Vel's voice. Then the tall white figure turned, and stood still, as if petrified.

Sea serpent; undated.

XI.

THE INN AT MASSALIA

Full of excellent food, lying comfortably on a soft bed with an enormous pillow at his back, Vel shamelessly let himself be spoiled by his father, who sat on a stool at the head of the bed and never seemed to have enough of gazing at him, stroking the hair off his forehead—how it had grown, in this short time!—and getting him to tell the whole story over again. Their meeting on the *Captain* had been so moving that once again, for the second time in his life, Vel had fainted, and his father had had to carry him like a child into the cabin. And then he had been quite firm that Vel must go straight to bed in the luxurious inn where he had taken lodgings when he arrived so dramatically in Massalia.

"But I'm quite all right now, Father," Vel kept saying impatiently. "I'm perfectly well and my leg hardly hurts at all. Tell me more about the *Captain*. When will she be ready to set sail? You still haven't told me a thing about the storm. Two masts have gone, I see."

"All three were weakened by the wind, and one fell into the sea. We were damaged, too, and dangerously, just above the waterline by a glancing blow from a rock, and lost two men, one of the sailors, and Sethre."

"Your helmsman! Oh, Father!"

"The gods of the sea were hungry this time, son. Hungry for human victims, and they chose the best. But fate wasn't altogether cruel. I've got you and I've got my old Ocno—I couldn't wish for anyone better than him. And the *Captain*'s cargo has been sold so profitably that we won't notice the loss of the *Boar* and we'll have Greek money to spare. No, as far as the money's concerned, we haven't really lost. But the dead —think of how many there were! Poseidon should be satisfied." He was silent, and shook his head bitterly, and Vel was silent too, not daring to ask his father more.

But Aules Pulena had lost none of his energy. "I must get back to the dock now. The innkeeper and his wife will look after you. I won't be back till evening. If we want to get the *Captain* repaired quickly I'm going to be busy. Luckily the port has very good equipment. Did you see the dock?"

"Father," said Vel beseechingly, "I haven't seen a thing. I've hardly seen the *Captain*. Let me come with you, I'm really perfectly well and I want to do what I can to help you."

Detail of the foot of a tomb; undated.

"All right, then! There's the cargo to check and I can't do it myself just now, when we have to get up the main mast. You and that giant you've brought along can watch the porters."

Vel happily flung back the blanket and put on the sandals his father had lent him, which were far too big. Aules laughed.

"Before we set sail I must buy you a few things in the market or your mother will think you're a beggar and won't recognize you. But don't think I'm buying you Phoenician purple or linen like your uncle's!"

When he heard his father joking Vel realized how happy he was, and his own joy bubbled over too. For the whole day he saw to the cargo with Ermor. Aules Pulena had been well paid for his linen, his elegant sandals, and in particular for the bronze and iron and the metal ore

from the workshops and mines of Populonia; in exchange for these he had gotten Greek copper coins, a
good many bars of Persian silver, and very valuable
goods such as soft leather, tanned and ready to be used
by the wonderful craftsmen of Tarquinia, whalebone,
and the furs of lynx, fox, and wolf brought from distant
lands in the north by nomad tribes in the forests. And
there were two grayish pebbles with a rough, uneven
surface, which were precious stones the Greeks called
electron, that came from the misty shores of the great
ocean where savage people gathered them on the beaches
and gave them to the enterprising traders who braved
the long journey into the interior. Vel took one of these
stones reverently in his hand. Seen thus, it was not at
all beautiful, and no one would have guessed that when
a skillful jeweler cut it it revealed a shiningly pure,
bright, transparent heart, or that a single piece of it,
finely polished and set in gold, was worth many slaves,
or even a small farm. The rich ladies of Tarquinia and
Cere and the Greek cities on the Great Sea all dreamed
of possessing a necklace made by the Etruscan jewelers
and adorned with the magical transparent stone. Vel
showed the two stones to Ermor before putting them
back in the leather bag, which was roughly made and
still had the characteristic stink of a badly tanned hide.
The Celt nodded. "It's the magic stone. I know it. My
people say these are the tears of the gods that fall to
earth. They're like no other stone!"

Vel put the bag back in his father's chest, which was
chained to the bunk in the cabin and had big bronze

locks. "Maybe these stones really are the tears of the gods," he said. "In any case, they're just as precious," he added, like a good practical merchant. And he forgot the electron at once and busied himself with the cargo.

The porters were local men, Ligurians and Iberians hired for two meals a day and a small sum to the sharp Greek contractor they worked for. They filed along the gangplank from the *Captain* to the quayside, bent under the poles of skins and leather that were her main cargo. Vel loved to see the goods piling up in the hold, filling it with a strong smell that others might have found disgusting but he thought very exciting—the smell of trade itself, of new countries, of people with habits and customs quite unlike those at home.

"I must ask Ermor to tell me about his country," he thought. "If only he were a bit chattier. But it takes a whole day to dig a few words out of him."

Working in the warm spring sunshine soon tired Vel, who was still convalescent, and he was glad when evening began falling over the great port and he went back to the inn with his father. The Ligurian innkeeper's hotel for rich merchants and important travelers was near the harbor in a rough, noisy district, built around a large paved courtyard with the kitchens, servants' rooms, stables and even two or three shops—a barber's, a potter's, a chandler's—opening onto it. The rooms for important visitors looked out onto another smaller courtyard, with a small green flower bed in it, tucked away inside the building and so much further from the street noises. This was a wise precaution, because Massalia was a lively place and the rumbling of carts in the narrow paved streets and the chatter of women going to the public fountains went on far into the night. There was a fountain at either end of the street in which stood the tavern, and both were very popular; the dockers cooked their supper on stoves which they often lit in the courtyards, and, depending on how tired they were, they would squabble, play dice, or sit in silence after a meal of cake, or boiled chick-peas; and the many wineshops, with stone benches facing onto the street, were filled with customers from early evening, arguing and shouting excitedly in several languages or in Greek mixed with Italian, Phoenician, Iberian, and Etruscan words.

After a large supper, served by the attentive innkeeper and several servants, Vel lay on his couch talking to his father. But he realized right away that Aules Pulena was uneasy. As he sipped his wine in its large goblet, sweetened with honey in the Greek manner, he kept looking at the door, or else staring thoughtfully at the marble floor.

"Are you expecting someone, Father?" Vel asked.

But just then the innkeeper came to the door, bowed and said someone was asking for the noble Etruscan merchant, Aules Pulena.

"Send him in," said Aules in Greek, and a small baldish man entered. He was respectably dressed, but Vel thought he must be a steward or administrator, that is, the high-ranking servant of a rich, noble house.

"Cele Aulenna sent me to greet you, noble Pulena," he said, bowing, "and wishes you to know his heart is joyful because the gods were good to you and gave you back your son."

Vel remembered the name of the merchant his father often mentioned, but he was surprised that he had not come himself to drink a goblet of wine with his friend, and had merely sent a servant—admittedly a superior one, but a servant nevertheless. It struck him as extremely discourteous and disrespectful, yet his father answered the man charmingly, offered him wine, and asked him to take his place on the third couch which was free. Then with a gesture he dismissed the inn-keeper's slaves, and when they had gone the servant spoke in a low voice.

"The noble merchant's ship is nearly ready, I believe?"

"Another two days' work: all we have to do is set up the third mast, which will take just two days," Aules answered, frowning.

"If you could manage it in a single day, that would be best, sir. Better work all night by torch light and leave at dawn the day after tomorrow."

Vel was longing to ask why it was so important to hurry, and what Cele Aulenna's servant really meant.

"Yes, sir," the man went on, "I'm sure you will understand that the wind will suit your sails best the day after tomorrow. This is what your friend Cele Aulenna sends me to say, together with his sincerest good wishes and a suckling lamb, whose blood will draw the sea gods' good will to you."

The man then poured a little of his wine on the floor

in honor of the gods, and drank off the rest, rose, bowed deeply, first to Aules, then to Vel, and went out of the room. The whole scene had taken only a few minutes. Aules sat up, yawning.

"Time for bed, son. I'll be on deck before dawn. Come along."

In their bedroom, which had two beds in it, a woman slave adjusted the wick of a small oil lamp and hung it up onto the ceiling. Aules began taking off his shoes and when she tried to help him he dismissed her. When they were alone he turned to Vel.

"I'm glad you haven't asked questions, although I could see you were longing to. You see, Massalia's not safe for us, and we've got to leave as fast as we possibly can. Cele Aulenna's a loyal friend, and a Tyrrhenian and a merchant besides. They held a meeting in the market place, in the Greek manner, and several speakers roused the people against us—against us Tyrrhenians, that is."

"But why?" Vel asked, astonished. "It's years since the battle of Alalia and all we want is to sell our goods in exchange for what they can give us."

"Yes, but you don't understand politics. Cele Aulenna and the other Tyrrhenian merchants in Massalia have nothing to fear for the moment. Our trade's important to the city and most people realize that. It will soon blow over, but every now and then something happens to stir up the people, a famine, say, or internal strife between the rich and powerful and the poor, or fighting with the tribes inland—and then the people's anger must find a victim to spend itself on. This time

we are the scapegoat, so we'll have to avoid trading with
Massalia for a while. There may even be a law to limit
the freedom of Tyrrhenians living here, making them
keep to their own districts, or increasing the taxes of
resident aliens—which means all foreigners who have
had permission to live on Greek territory. But the *Captain's* nearly ready, and in another day we'll be sea-
worthy again. I wanted to make the gods a sacrifice that
would be worthy of your extraordinary survival, but
we'll have to do it at Populonia. The gods can't be angry
when it's not our fault. Now, go to sleep!"

Populonia! Vel had hardly thought of it lately. He
had thought much more of Tarquinia, of his mother
and even old Ninia. Now, he remembered Seia with
pleasure. They would travel to Tarquinia together and
he would have plenty of time to tell her about his ad-
ventures. And wouldn't she be amazed! He thought se-
cretly—wouldn't she admire him! Tomorrow he'd surely
have a moment to go to the market and buy her a present with his mother's coins, which had miraculously
survived the storm. And with this agreeable thought he
dropped off to sleep and never heard his father when he
got up to go to the *Captain*.

But when he got up himself, he found he could get on
quite well, in spite of being alone, by talking to the
Ligurian innkeeper in the kind of Greek Ibico would
have turned up his nose at—in fact even whipped Vel
for using, a Greek that was getting to be more and more
like Ocno's. The innkeeper agreed to take Vel to the
market and asked what he wanted to buy, but Vel

carefully refrained from telling him how much money he had, and showed him just one of his coins.

"Well, sir," said the innkeeper, bowing, "a didrachma from Taranto will certainly buy something fine. And when you have done your shopping you won't have to be taken to the ship, because the market is almost down by the sea."

In fact, with the hills pressing down behind Massalia, there was not a great deal of space for houses and shops. The more elegant houses, and the villas of the city authorities and rich merchants, were built on the hills around the bay, and gleamed white among the dark green Mediterranean woods.

Vel, the innkeeper, and two slaves carrying large baskets for the day's shopping, went through the crowded, narrow streets. No one took any notice of them. The innkeeper just greeted a few shopkeepers already sitting at their counters. The market was in the square used for public meetings, where decisions taken for the general good were discussed in the presence of most of the population—as was the case in many Greek cities. Merchants of various nationalities had shops all around the square, and Vel knew that Cele Aulenna's must be one of them. But the innkeeper led him to a corner, and through a small porch with two narrow columns where a fat merchant with a luxuriant black beard, was squatting crosslegged at a door, giving orders to a couple of slaves hanging bright fabrics around the door post, and obviously not too pleased with the effect they were achieving. When the innkeeper came up to him the merchant leaped up at once and greeted Vel very politely in Greek, his small black eyes taking in the boy's ragged clothes and outsize sandals, though he asked no awkward questions. In fact, as soon as the innkeeper explained that Vel was looking for a fine present to take home from his journey and that he would pay in a silver coin minted at Taranto, the Phoenician never stopped bowing. Then he went ahead of them into the shop, clapping his hands, and an old slave ran in from a room at the back—obviously the storeroom—and listened humbly to his master giving a flood of orders in Carthaginian. He left and came back carrying some small jewel cases and tiny bronze tripods that held small pots made of glazed clay and carefully sealed with wax in a ring.

"Young sir," said the merchant, with a glance at Vel's

Head of a bronze statue of a youth;
5th Century B.C.

ring, "noble sir, here is a choice selection of the best perfumes, which would delight divine nostrils! They are the fruit of Egyptian wisdom, distilled in the East. Any lady of a great house would be prepared to pay many Persian coins of purest silver for one of these little jars . . . and pray observe the valuable jar itself, which reflects all the colors of the rainbow in its glazed clay— why, it is worth even more than its contents, and we Phoenicians, may Baal forgive me if I lie, learned the way to make jars of this kind directly from the gods . . ."

Vel had picked up one of the frail little jars and was looking at it dubiously, shaking his head as he had seen his father do when bargaining, to show he thought little of the goods he had before him.

"No?" said the Phoenician, watching him. "Perhaps you don't want perfume? Then, as I see you want something more valuable—although Massalia specializes in these scented unguents—I'll show you something really wonderful, more so than anything you can have seen in your young life—if you'll forgive my saying so, sir."

So saying, he opened one of the jewel boxes made of fragrant wood, and, being deliberately slow, took out a finely chased gold pin. Vel frowned at the sight of it; why, wasn't it . . . wasn't it . . . yes, it was! He recognized the box and the pin, which was decorated with an engraving of doves. It was one of the pieces of jewelry his father had brought from Tarquinia, and he had often seen it when he was looking through the most valuable part of the cargo. The Phoenician mistook his interest for a wish to buy.

"Ah, I see you have subtle taste already, noble sir, in spite of your youth. This is a masterpiece of Etruscan art and I've had it only a week. But alas, I don't want to offend you—may Hermes save me from doing so!—but this piece of jewelry is priceless and I'm afraid less than five didrachmas . . . no, I'm afraid I couldn't part with it for less!"

Vel burst out laughing.

"Five didrachmas! I'll ask my father how much you gave him for this pin, and may I be flayed alive if you gave more than two. You needn't invoke Hermes, Phoenician! I'm not Greek, even though I have Tarantine money."

For a moment the Phoenician seemed confused; then he caressed his beard and smiled.

"Ah, so it's the Pulena leopards on that seal! If my eyes weren't suffering from these morning fogs which affect them, I would have recognized them right away. But if you think I paid such a paltry sum for this masterpiece, you're wrong . . ."

"Yes, yes—but I'd sooner have one of the little jars."

"Of course, of course!" Seeing that the deal had not fallen through after all, the Phoenician was in good humor again. "Seeing you're a merchant and the son of a great merchant, and Etruscan as well, which means you're as unpopular here as we are, I'll make it a bargain. Ah, the ingratitude of men! Who made Massalia prosperous and rich? Why, the Phoenicians and the Etruscans—eh, innkeeper?"

"Well, I'm Ligurian myself and all I wish is that the

taxes for foreign residents wouldn't be raised every year. These Greeks are too good at squeezing us—they think we're like magic vines that will give wine forever."

"That's it, that's it! You're perfectly right, my friend. But for this very reason, I'll ask a ridiculous price for this valuable unguent—a really laughable price—a didrachma for a small jar—now, how about this one?"

Of course Vel had no intention of accepting this, and offered half a didrachma for two jars. The merchant then pretended to tear his beard, and tearfully invoked any number of Phoenician divinities, and after all this Vel managed to get two jars for one didrachma and the esteem of the Phoenician, who predicted a splendid future for him as a merchant—or rather as a strangler, which was the highest compliment he could pay him.

As soon as they were outside the square, the innkeeper spoke.

"Well, I've lost alot of time, sir, but it was well worth it," he said. "But you'll have to get to the repair dock on your own. Anyway, you can see the masts of the ship and her sails from here."

Vel nodded, and the innkeeper set off for the end of the square where peasants and fishermen were offering their wares, followed by the two slaves with the baskets. The dock was close by and Vel, delighted with what he had bought and the price he had beaten the Phoenician down to, hurried over to the ship with his precious jars, not stopping once in the streets which were now seething with people.

They were working frantically on the *Captain*. Aules

Pulena was directing the work of caulkers, carpenters, and sailors. The main mast was already in place and the mizzen mast had only to have the crossbar which would hold the sail in place. Ocno was seeing to the minor repairs and in particular to the rudder; he would be taking the place of the dead Sethre on the return journey and he told Vel not to get in the way because "he wanted to check with his eye whatever he was going to use with his hands."

About midday a few idlers gathered on the wharf watching the work curiously, yet looking very unfriendly. Aules gave no sign that he had noticed, but his face darkened. Before leaving the ship with Vel to go back to the inn, he talked to Ocno for some time and, roaming about not far from the pair of them, Vel heard the words "men," "armed," and "ready" several times. To his great disappointment they did not even pass through the market on their way back. "The innkeeper's eldest son is the same age as you," Aules said. "We'll buy his best clothes and a pair of his sandals."

Vel was not too pleased at the idea. He wanted to arrive at Populonia looking his best. But then he consoled himself by taking another look at the Phoenician merchant's jars, which seemed to him a very fine present, just right for a young lady. They crossed the wharf, pushing through the crowd still thick on the quayside, which made no effort to move away as they passed and almost forced them to shove through. They heard a muttering, not loud but angry, like the menacing buzz when a hornet's nest is disturbed. Vel was beginning to be scared, but the four stout sailors with them looked so muscular and so determined that nothing happened until they slipped through the open door of the inn, which shut behind them in a flash.

Supper was soon over. Vel had been very hungry after his busy afternoon. In bed he realized his father was unable to sleep, but dared not ask questions. In any case, he knew quite well what was worrying him. He was afraid that some fanatic would lead an attack on the inn or that a Greek ship would actually stop them before they managed to set sail. But the *Captain* was ready and dawn would come soon. The entire crew was on board that night, and though no one was allowed to stay ashore for any reason at all, there had been no grumbling. Everyone understood the gravity of the situation. Yet Vel had caught his father's anxiety and could not sleep either. At last he dozed off, but after what seemed to him a very short time he leaped out of bed with a cry, his heart beating hard. The innkeeper was banging on the door and in a low, terrified voice kept saying,

"Hurry, sir, hurry, by all the gods!"

It was a matter of moments. Vel found himself racing through the streets behind his father, wearing the clothes of the innkeeper's son and carrying a bundle on his back. The good Ligurian had warned them just in time. When they reached the *Captain* in the pale moonlight, black figures leaned over the ship's side. Vel and his father leaped up the gangplank and the moment they set foot on board the oars dipped simultaneously into the water, and, in complete silence with its lights out, the *Captain* moved slowly away from the wharf. There was no time even to pull in the gangplank, which fell into the water; all they could hear was the creaking of the winch still pulling up the anchor while the ship was in motion.

The whole thing had been perfectly timed. In the streets of Massalia torches were flaming and in a moment a group of shouting men appeared on the wharf. But the *Captain* was now moving fast, its oars dipping in a faster rhythm. Vel, holding the deck rail astern, could already see the whole sweep of the harbor, while the dark hulk of one of the three big islands that shut it in on the southwest drew nearer, growing larger and larger on the bow.

Ocno was using one of the stroke oars angrily, nervous at the shallowness of the water, and grunting orders quickly to the mate, who was gripping the other oar. Aules Pulena stood well balanced, straddling slightly, arms crossed, staring at the retreating shore for a long time. Then he turned his back on it and gave an order,

"Lights out till we're out of the harbor." And he looked down at the ladder that led to the rows of oarsmen.

XII.

TERROR AT SEA

For the whole day after their flight from Massalia, and for most of the following night, there was no wind. But no danger threatened from the city. The oars dipped in a regular rhythm, the oarsmen taking turns. While one team bent their sweating backs, rowing vigorously, the men in the other team rested, their heads pillowed on their arms which were flung across their unused oars. But toward morning a fresh wind rose from the north and the sails bellied out like white apple blossoms. Aules peered up at the masts and crossbars, shrouds and sails, listening carefully to every squeak he thought suspicious but the repairs did not seem to have suffered from being done so fast, and the *Captain* sailed on, majestic and elegant. Under the main mast, Vel listened happily to the rustle of the bellying sails, and his blood

ran faster, as it always did when he heard it. The breeze
flung the salt spray onto his lips and he licked them,
delighted to taste the flavor like none other, however
delicious, and felt he had found an old friend. The wind
blew toward the east until halfway through the second
day, and then instead of dropping, it veered to the
southwest and, weighed down by her cargo and hampered by this contrary wind, the *Captain* started moving
much more slowly. The whole crew was on deck, and
Aules Pulena cupped his hands around his mouth and
shouted orders to the sailors, who were climbing up the
masts like monkeys to slacken one sail or strike another.
The wind was doing its best to blow them off course and
the sails had to be cleverly managed to prevent this. Yet
the *Captain,* though moving slowly, continued to be
blown off course. They should have been following the
coastline for a long way yet, and instead they lost sight
of it almost at once, which showed quite clearly that
they were being dragged southward. Vel, his hair flung
into his eyes by the wind, went astern to see Ocno who
was still at the rudder.

"We're being blown out to sea, aren't we?" he shouted
above the noise of the wind.

"Doesn't matter. We're almost at the eastern island
where we'd have had to turn south for Corsica in any
case."

But the wind showed no sign of dropping, although
the sky stayed calm. It blew almost constantly for the
whole evening, dragging the *Captain* farther and farther
southwest. It was a weary night. Aules Pulena had to

hand over to the mate for a few hours, cursing fate for
taking the excellent Sethre, so there was no one to take
over from poor Ocno, who hung on, gritting his teeth,
and at the end of his tether. Sail had been reduced as
much as possible to give the gusty wind less of a chance,
but when the wind dropped at last, at sunrise, the men
were exhausted. Aules thought it a good idea to discuss
things in his cabin and sent for Ocno and the mate. Vel
followed them, and his father did not send him away. In
fact he made him sit down beside him, and Vel felt so
proud that he forgot his sleepiness, weariness, and hun-
ger. For some hours no one had had time to prepare
meals, and dry biscuit, however nutritious, was not exactly appetizing.

"We're a good way off course," said Aules Pulena,
"but the trouble is I don't know how far west the wind
blew us."

The mate was a man of few words, but his advice was
always worth having.

"All we can do is go northeast using the oars, sir. The
bit of wind that's left us is blowing us in the right direction, but we can't make much use of it. Besides, the
oarsmen are the only men on board who aren't exhausted, and they can row pretty fast now."

"Yes, we'll be a couple of days behind, that's all,"
said Ocno. "But one thing's sure for the moment, and
it's a very great deal. There's no danger of storms. Instead of bringing stormy weather, the wind has swept
the sky clear. In a couple of days we'll meet the currents
near Corsica . . ."

A long shout from the deck interrupted him.

"What is it? I didn't hear!" said Aules.

"Sail to port, Father," said Vel.

The three men leaped up.

"A sail? But we're completely off all the routes."

"Someone else blown off course, like us," Vel suggested, but no one listened. Aules was already under the main mast, shouting to the lookout at the masthead. The man was down in a flash and in a few breathless words explained.

"A single triangular sail, sir. A small ship—very fast."

"And her flag?" asked Aules. "Didn't you see the flag?"

"Well, I don't think there was one, sir. No, I'm sure there wasn't. She's not a cargo ship, for sure, and she's not a warship either, and you can't even see whether she's Greek or Phoenician. The only thing is, she's very fast. A few minutes ago the sail was just a dot from the masthead, and now you can see it from here—look, sir!"

Vel saw his father and Ocno exchanging a look and could not think why, but an uneasy shiver ran down his spine.

"Go on up again," Aules told the lookout, "and answer my questions as exactly as you can."

The man, who was extremely agile, was on the crossbar of the main mast in a moment.

"It's coming toward us, sir," he shouted at once. "But I still can't see a flag!"

Aules gave no answer. The sail was now visible from

the deck and after a very few minutes the small, very slender hull appeared, growing larger and larger to the naked eye. It was rowed by a single line of oarsmen.

"But why do they keep up that rowing rhythm?" Vel wondered. "They'll ram us. You'd think they were racing!"

There was something strange and evil about the ship approaching the scarcely moving *Captain* in perfect silence, swift as an arrow. The crew watched it without moving, some at the ship's side, some on deck, all fascinated, almost spellbound. Suddenly Aules Pulena's voice broke the silence.

"Row hard, if you value your lives!" he shouted. "Arm yourselves, men! They're after us!"

Chaos and confusion followed. Vel had scarcely taken in what was happening and gaped in bewilderment at the men swarming about the deck. He heard Ocno roar down the hatchway to the ranks of oarsmen. Like a flame a single word spread around the *Captain* and Vel heard it clearly.

"Pirates, pirates!"

"Pirates!" Vel repeated. "It can't be!"

His father dragged him into the cabin.

"Father, what are we to do?" Vel panted, his belly contracted with terror, making it almost impossible to speak.

"Try and escape," said Aules, his face dark.

The *Captain* was gathering speed. At first her heaviness hampered her, then it became an advantage.

"Suppose we can't? Suppose they catch us?"

"Then we'll put up a fight—we've got axes, knives, swords, arrows . . ."

Vel's eyes opened wide, but he said nothing. His mind was full of images of blood and terror. Ocno, who spoke very knowingly about them, had told him dozens of stories about pirates. Everyone in Tarquinia suspected that this now peaceable, honest sailor had been a pirate when he was young. Vel himself believed it. So he believed firmly in the sea robbers' terrible reputation for cruelty. Every ship seized was sent pitilessly to the bottom with all its crew—at least with those who had not been killed in the fight—when there was a fight. The pirates must leave no witnesses, for they were bandits pursued by all the coastal towns throughout the Great Sea.

Aules Pulena realized what was going on in his son's head, and shouted, "Here, Vel, I need you! The men are trying to catch all the wind they can—we've got to arm them. Come on!"

As his father had realized it would, the need to do something stimulated Vel and made him forget his terror. In a moment they were down in the hold; the oarsmen were bent over their oars, their backs arched, their muscles standing out with the effort and gleaming with sweat; they neither spoke nor looked up. At such a time silence was enforced, and the overseer was ready to flog mercilessly anyone who dared open his mouth—his stout oxhide whip was long enough to reach any oarsman in the team. Vel and his father dashed down the gangway between the oarsmen and plunged into the dark hold. They came out loaded with weapons, for Aules had prudently kept back some of the cargo taken on at Populonia, although when he thought of using the bronze knives it was more a Greek ambush at Massalia that he had in mind than an attack by pirates. Up on deck Vel ran from man to man handing out weapons. He could not fail to feel proud of the crew's discipline. No one was distracted from what he had to do, no one even seemed to realize the danger, or at least to want to notice it. But even the youngest and most timid held their weapons stoutly. They might not all be fighters, but they all knew what a pirate attack meant. Vel made four or five trips to the armory and each time he came back on deck he told himself not to look at the sea, yet never managed to avoid doing so. The *Captain* was now moving very fast, but the small light vessel in pursuit seemed to fly over the calm water. Not a voice was heard. Ocno, at the rudder, leather cap jammed down on his head, laughed joylessly when Vel brought him a big double-edged sword.

"I prefer my own!" he said.

And tied to a leather halter hung around Ocno's neck, to leave his hands free, Vel saw a long curved blade with a horn handle. A knife was stuck into his belt as well and he was glaring fiercely at the approaching pirate ship.

"Ocno," Vel asked softly, not knowing quite why he was whispering. "Why are they so quiet? They're near us now and if they shouted we'd hear them."

"Ah, you'll hear them, you'll hear them, never fear," said Ocno bitterly. "They're saving their breath for when they board us. As soon as they start the assault you'll hear them screaming like all the monsters of Aita."

"Ocno," said Vel, staring at the sea to avoid looking Ocno in the face. "They're nearly on us. I'm frightened!"

"So am I," said the old man simply. "But so are they, you can be sure of that. There aren't many of them— there can't be more than thirty or thirty-five. And we're more than seventy—including the oarsmen, admittedly . . ."

But before he had finished the sentence Vel had shot away. He had an idea, an idea he thought stupendous. He ran down to the hold again, but had hardly reached the rows of oarsmen when a great thud hurled him headlong at the overseer's feet. The oarsmens' screams of terror rose above a dry splintering noise, and the overseer flung himself between the rows, flogging the men madly, but in vain. Vel saw all the left-hand oars shoot in suddenly from the side, knocking the oarsmen wildly off their benches. On deck, blood-curdling shrieks broke out, and Vel and the overseer, who flung away his useless whip, shot up the ladder again, the big man clutching an old double battle-ax while Vel drew the sword he had chosen from its scabbard. Its blade was light but well tempered. On deck, the confusion had calmed down. The pirate ship had not grappled with the *Captain*, because Ocno had cleverly managed to swerve at the last minute; she had merely brushed violently against the *Captain*'s side, snapping off her own oars and the *Captain*'s as if they were made of straw. So now the two ships were side by side, bumping each other like two great ducks playing in a pond, and the pirates had to jump off their own rigging onto the *Captain*'s deck. Aules and all the sailors had rushed to starboard, and the first two pirates to jump, ragged, bearded, and black as devils from beyond the grave, lay dead on the deck, stabbed by a dozen swords. Vel saw a shining pool of blood spreading under their two bodies, and realized he was standing there staring stupidly and feeling no horror at all.

"Look out! Aft!" yelled Ocno at that moment.

The pirates were trying to hook a rope gangway onto the *Captain* from their ship, and so climb over the *Captain*'s side.

"Father!" cried Vel. He wanted to ask him what he thought of his idea, but Aules Pulena leaped into the bow followed by the oarsmen's overseer, whirling his battle-ax, and by Ocno, and for a while wild confusion raged around the place where the pirates had hooked on their gangway bridge. Just then a very athletic pirate tried to jump from his own mainsail on to the *Captain*'s mizzen-mast, but he missed it and, with a shriek of terror that chilled poor Vel, hit the edge of the ship's side and fell into the sea. Forward, there was a jolt. A second gangway had been hooked on to the *Captain*. Only two or three of the *Captain*'s crew had seen the danger and dashed across—the swarm of shouting pi-

Wall painting; 4th Century B.C.

rates would soon overwhelm them. Vel no longer hesitated—there was no time to lose. With the fight now raging on deck, he leaped down into the hold. As he ran down the gangway between the oarsmen, he heard them shouting and pulling at their chains with all their strength, though in vain. They knew the pirates would let them sink with the ship, without giving them a thought. Vel opened the door of the hold, and, in a single leap, was over at the overseer's bench. He knew the key of the men's fetters must be there under the drum used to give them the rhythm for rowing. The *Captain* was now moving slowly, dragging the pirate ship with her, and Vel kept losing his balance, but at last he found the key and waved it in the air. The oarsmen shouted, all together; then were silent. Gaping with astonishment, they stared at the pale boy waving the key. Was he holding a chance of salvation for them? In the sudden silence they heard the uproar on deck, the clashing of swords.

"Men!" cried Vel, his voice breaking into a nervous sob. "If the pirates beat us we'll all be killed. I'm going to free you. There are weapons over there. Will you fight?"

He did not wait for an answer, and knew he was running a terrible risk. These wretched slaves, the dregs of the marketplace, brutalized by the harshness of their life, might even surrender to the pirates, hoping to be taken into their band, or simply try to escape in the boats and save their lives without a thought for their owners or the ship. But his unbelievable action seemed to get the result he hoped for.

"Free us! Free us and we'll fight! Free us, you brave lad!" they yelled, in all sorts of languages. Vel was frantically busy. The first slaves freed grabbed the first weapons they could find, and a few stayed behind to help Vel. Then a compact group of about forty men suddenly burst up out of the hold. The pirates were all over the deck, and in ten or twenty places men were fighting for their lives. Shrieking, the oarsmen fell on the pirates.

With his back to the cabin door and his sword pointing straight ahead of him, Vel could not take in what was happening. Then Ocno whirled before him, furiously staunching the blood that was pouring from a wound in his face and blinding him. But he had crossed swords with one of the pirates and the two of them disappeared behind the main mast. Aules Pulena's white cloak was near the side of the ship, stained with great splashes of blood. Whose blood? Vel tried to join him, but one of the oarsmen rushed up to him with a pirate at his heels, desperately trying to defend himself from his enemy's sword with a knife that was far too short. Vel, overcome with rage, dashed up to the two fighters and plunged his sword with all his strength into the pirate's side. The blade went through his ribs absurdly easily, and Vel immediately dropped the hilt, as if it were red-hot. Strangely enough, this coincided exactly with the end of battle. Most of the pirates who had boarded the *Captain* lay dead on the deck. The oarsmen, bursting from the hold, had swayed the fight in a few minutes. Only about a dozen pirates managed to escape to their own ship, and immediately hacked at the gangway that still joined them to the *Captain* with their axes.

"Follow them! follow them!" cried Aules Pulena, but the pirate ship had already moved away from the *Captain*'s side and several yards immediately yawned between the two ships. No one dared obey him. Then suddenly, one, two, ten flaming arrows flew into the enemy's sails. Two oarsmen, kneeling on deck, were tirelessly shooting, while their comrades feverishly prepared the arrows and held them out to them. One by one they ripped through the sails of the pirate ship, burning through the air like wicked tongues, one after another.

"To the oars!" Aules Pulena now ordered. "Pull away as fast as you can!"

Without a word, the slaves flung themselves onto their benches. Vel and the others stayed on deck, gazing fascinated at the enemy ship, on which the few men who had escaped could not control the fire flaring up from those arrows soaked in pitch. Their fate was now sealed with that of the ship; they must either burn with it, or jump into the sea.

Aules Pulena gave an order.

"Pick none of them up! Leave them to the fishes!"

Vel's heart contracted with pity, and a sob escaped him. Ocno, still panting, his wild gray hair soaked with blood, glared fiercely at him. The boy realized he could say nothing: in any case those men knew the pitiless law of the sea. They had committed many murders, and even if they had been picked up and taken to Tarquinia, their fate would still have been terrible.

The *Captain* was pulling away fast, in spite of being unevenly rowed. Vel thought he would never in his whole life forget the screams of the pirates imprisoned on their ship, adrift and burning like a funeral pyre.

But when he timidly approached his father, to seek comfort beside him, he saw that Aules Pulena's face had grown very pale, and that he was trying to keep on his feet by clinging to a rope at the main mast. He realized suddenly that his father was wounded. Aules smiled at him.

"It was you who saved us, Vel, I'm proud of you . . ."

Vel tried to answer, but no sound came from his open lips. Frozen with fear, he saw the tall white figure bending further and further forward, slowly slipping onto the deck, and then, without a groan, lying there very still.

XIII.

AT HOME

The sun was gilding the terraces of Tarquinia and in the Pulena's courtyard a nervous black horse harnessed to the town carriage was pawing the ground. Ermor stroked the trembling muscles along its shining mane, which was cut short like the crest of a helmet. He was in love with this splendid creature, who was so different from the small, stringy ponies in the woods where he came from.

"I bet you and that horse have had some cozy chats together! I don't know whether you've learned to neigh or whether he's learned to speak Celtic."

Ermor jumped, rather shamefacedly, but did not seem to mind the joke. "Horses are good," he said, in his usual abrupt way. "They're good friends!"

"Better than people, you mean? Well, share your

bed with him, if you like. My father says he's never seen anyone with a touch like you, when it comes to horses. And here he is now!"

Aules Pulena had appeared under the courtyard loggia, and at the sight of his son he smiled. Ermor held the reins till the two of them had climbed into the light, two-wheeled carriage and then threw them to Aules.

"You won't make him go too hard, will you? He had a bit of a cough last night, and . . ."

Anyone else who dared to suggest something of the kind would have received a sharp retort from Aules Pulena, but since it was Ermor he spoke reassuringly.

"Don't worry, Ermor, we're not going far."

The wheels rattled over the paved courtyard, and the carriage went through the narrow gateposts and was soon in the square. Vel kept his balance with difficulty by holding onto the painted wooden edge of the side, and although he was very curious to know the object of this trip, he asked no questions. Aules had simply told him to be ready and he had no idea where they were going. It was unusual not to have Ermor with them. The Celt had given up none of his old habits—his taciturnity, his hair in pigtails, his barbarian clothes, but in the four moons since their return, he had become very useful around the house and everyone thought well of him. His great love for horses made him a wonderful groom and coachman. Vel smiled to himself. Already his mother and Seia trusted no one else to take them on their trips into town or to the temple, and this had stirred up some trouble with the older servants. But Ermor

Bronze relief on the Monteleme Chariot; 550 B.C.

with his steely blue eyes, managed to arouse a respect that was very much like superstitious fear—even in old Ninia. Besides, the ladies often went out in litters as well, and then the old slaves got their own back, because Ermor completely refused to become "a beast of burden".

The carriage had gone fast down the steep hill, and was now running beside the trickle of a river that had almost dried up in the summer heat; soon it came to the foot of a stiff hill. Aules Pulena took both reins in his right hand and patted his son's shoulder affectionately.

"I bet a couple of new dice I can guess what you're thinking!"

Vel shook his head, smiling.

"I can! You're wondering where we're going."

"Wrong!" exclaimed Vel, delightedly. "You've lost! I was thinking of Ermor, and the horses, and mother . . ."

"Right, you've won your pair of dice."

"Oh, but I'm also curious to know where we're going, Father. By all the million tritons of the abyss," he said, using one of Ocno's favorite expressions, "I swear I'm dying of curiosity."

"Well then, here you are!"

They had reached a junction that divided the dusty road into two narrower paths: one went along by the sea, following the course of the stream they had just crossed; the other went up the slope and wound around to the top of the hill.

"The city of the dead!" Vel exclaimed. "Why are we going there?"

Aules Pulena dropped the reins since the horse began walking more slowly and regularly.

"The journey we took taught you a great deal, Vel. And you behaved very well throughout it. You were brave, without becoming hardhearted, and that's what makes a boy into a man. But it taught me something, too."

"You, Father?"

"Are you surprised? It's quite natural, though, and when your time comes you'll feel just the same. Before the journey to Massalia you were a child, a puppy, a little spoiled by your mother and the slaves . . . Yes, it's no good protesting!"

Vel turned red, but Aules took no notice.

"This single journey has made a man of you, and at the same time it has shown me I'm no longer as young and strong as I was. When children grow up, parents start to decline; they walk down the road their sons are beginning to climb."

Vel glanced furtively at his father. He feared, and knew, that these words were covering something else. After the pirates' attack, the wound in his back had immobilized Aules Pulena for two moons, and the doctors of Tarquinia had said frankly that he would never be completely well again. Everyone at home seemed to be part of a loving conspiracy. From the slaves to Vel's mother and old Ninia, no one ever mentioned illnesses and medicines, no one seemed to notice that his father grew steadily paler and thinner and wearier. But Vel knew, like everyone else; and the pain of hiding his doubts and fears was maturing him, making him grow up even faster than the adventurous voyage to Massalia.

But sometimes at night he was obsessed by a nightmare, and it was always the same. It was not frightening, only infinitely sad. The yellow, fever-ridden face of the soothsayer at Populonia shaking his head and saying, "I see nothing to show your return . . ."

"And that's why we've come here," Aules Pulena continued. "In any case, I should have started preparing my resting place which will be where all the Pulenas are laid."

The carriage was now moving along a narrow road that ran from south to northwest over the whole length of the hill between Tarquinia and the sea. Tall plants, swept over by the salt wind that blew in from the calm, glittering sea lay on either side of it, and even in early summer the breeze kept combing through the asphodels that grew thickly up there, and brought the harsh smell of the waves inland. On either side of the road and over the whole gentle slope of the hill there were small, scarcely noticeable grassy domes. Aules stopped the carriage near the road, tied the bridle to a ball-handle on the carriage, and jumped down. Vel followed him, in silence. Every small dome had a door; the one where Aules Pulena stopped was open, and two quiet voices came up from below, the word "master" recurring in the conversation. The Pulenas went down a slippery slope, into which rough steps had been cut, and entered an underground room with a roof that sloped from a central beam. One of the two men inside, a small, bearded, paint-stained man, greeted Aules Pulena. Vel knew he was a famous painter, sought by the best families in Tarquinia, and was surprised to see how shabbily he was dressed. Yet painters in Tarquinia were a rich, powerful group. Aules returned his greeting with dignity and courtesy.

"Greetings, Tuna Calinna. My son and I are anxious to admire the images you create with your wonderful brush."

The work had started barely a month before, and so far three of the walls had only the background of white plaster on which the pictures would be painted. On the wall at the end there was a sketch in brick red of the sacred gate through which the spirits passed to enter the kingdom of Aita. On the earthly side of the gate, the living were celebrating the dead person's departure with funeral games.

Vel went straight over to the fourth wall, which was on the left of the entrance. Two torches, fixed in corners of the cell, lit it up brightly. Tuna Calinna seemed flattered by the boy's astonishment.

"Do you like my picture, then?"

Vel nodded several times, unable to speak. The whole length of the wall was covered with a seascape, full of people who looked extraordinarily alive. There was the *Captain*, with its three masts, its rigging and its sails, and on deck, men were busy getting ready to sail. Vel could almost hear the lapping of the water on the hull,

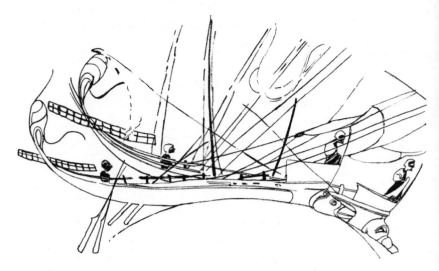

Etruscan ships painted on pottery; undated.

and although the sky was only sketched in with a few blue brush-strokes, it already looked like a great open space.

The painter seemed delighted at Vel's surprise; then suddenly his mood changed. He called his assistant—a large, placid youth—a number of rude names, and, as if seized by some sudden fit, hurled himself on his brushes. Bounding about on his short legs, and touching the wall with paint here and there, he took no notice of the Pulenas. Aules Pulena took Vel by the arm and led him outside.

"Come," he said. "His genius is tormenting him; he can now see and hear nothing but its voice."

As soon as they were out in the dazzling light, they stopped to gaze at the endless stretch of sea that melted into an incandescent mist on the horizon.

Vel felt very close to his father, spiritually closer than

he had ever felt before. So he ventured to express a thought that he had never yet put into words.

"Father," he said, "I think everyone has a genius that tells him what to do and urges him on and won't let him rest. Like Achilles, who was always seeking battles, or the divine Ulysses . . ."

"Or like Ocno and Ermor, or even Tulumnes and your Uncle Larnth, in their way; like your father and now like you yourself. Yes, everyone has his genius to urge him on towards something and give him no peace till he has won it. But I'm glad you mentioned Achilles and Ulysses, and called only Ulysses 'divine'. Because our genius is the same as his, dear Vel. The genius that sends us to sea, among new peoples and new lands, whether civilized or savage."

"Is that why there's a ship on the wall of our house beyond?" Vel asked.

Aules Pulena was looking at the sea, with a melancholy smile.

"Anyone who sees it," he replied, "will know the Pulenas were good sons of Tarquinia, mother of all the Tyrrhenian people on the coast, and that they lived and died for the sea alone."

HISTORICAL NOTE

We know that the Etruscans were a highly civilized people who lived in Italy in pre-Christian times, but they disappeared over two thousand years ago and for most of that time their secret has remained hidden. Their origins are mysterious, their language is undeciphered, and few events in their history are known. Yet perhaps no other people has worked on the imagination of amateur researchers as they have done, or has aroused such greed in those who sacked their tombs, or such interest in scholars throughout the world.

From the River Po to the Tiber, in Tuscany, Umbria, Latium, Emilia, and Campania, there are tangible signs of the presence of the Etruscans. They cannot vanish completely into dust, for their small towns are built on hills of tufa and alabaster, with walls of perfectly square-cut stones, and doorways with arches of remarkable strength and proportions: majestic, calm, silent "cities of the dead". In the peasants' houses, even today, you may find exquisitely made small pots and amphorae used in the kitchen: they have been ploughed up in the fields and now stand on top of the stove, which is made of a single, handcut block of stone and is itself a direct descendant of the Etruscans' ancestral hearth.

Perhaps this is what is so fascinating about the Etruscans: they do not live on merely in museums full of splendid jewels, vases and weapons, or in proud monuments from a warlike past, like the Romans with their triumphal columns and arches. The Etruscans have a quieter way of making themselves known, through beautiful, peaceable, useful objects that tell us what really mattered in their lives: streets, the remains of which were paved by the Romans and still lie beneath today's asphalt; gates and aqueducts; walls and drains. There are even—recently discovered by aerial photography— networks of canals that show an astonishingly well developed system of irrigation and agriculture.

The tombs of the Etruscans are unique, unlike any others. Now that the great cupolas at Cere and the small underground rooms with sloping roofs at Tarquinia have been cleared of the objects that have been taken to museums, we can see the Etruscans more clearly in these last homes of theirs, for in the tombs, in glowing colors, they painted all their love of life.

In these paintings are banquets, where friends lie on soft couches talking together; circus games, in which athletes show their delight in youth and strength and agility; and chariot races, in which men and their horses strive together for victory.

Scholars are still trying to understand the Etruscan language and what they are hoping to discover one day is an inscription in two languages which will give them the key to the secret. Then perhaps they will find out more about the Etruscans themselves. But what we already have—their paintings and the objects they made and used—is enough to give us an exact and fascinating picture of the merchants and sailors, artists and artisans, farmers and laborers, doctors and wise men, local chiefs and priests, and their life on the shores of the Tyrrhenian sea.

ABOUT THE AUTHOR

Giuliana Pandolfi Boldrini was born in Florence in 1934. She studied classics at Universita degli Studi in Florence, where she obtained her degree in 1953 with a thesis on Sophocles. She is now a teacher and, since the death of her husband, has been living in the country outside Florence.

THE ETRUSCAN LEOPARDS, which was published in Italy in 1965, is her first book for young people. The idea for it grew out of her deep interest in the Etruscans and their way of life.